Moments of –
Distraction,
Redemption,
and *Desire*

Moments of – Distraction, Redemption, and *Desire*

©2024 Jen K. Ludwig

ISBN-13: 978 1 60571 653 4

Printed in the United States of America.

Moments of –
Distraction,
Redemption, and
Desire

Jen K. Ludwig

Dedication

To my father, Wolfgang Ludwig.
You have been with me every step of the way,
even now, I know you are still with me.
I love you Dad.

He lay back on his bed, the metal springs recoiling as they shifted under his weight. He raised his arms and folded his hands behind his head, staring at the ceiling. It was 1 a.m. and he was wideawake. The lights from the city traffic illuminated the windowpane, making shadows of bars on the ceiling. He was used to the noise of the city and welcomed it tonight, hoping it would replace his thoughts, but there was no reprieve. His eyes barely blinking, his breath steady. He took in a deep breath, feeling his chest expand, then he let it out. She was beautiful.

Zander replayed in his mind walking up her drive. It was a warm day, few of them left, as the seasons were changing. On the property stood an old Victorian house, a horse barn with a hayloft, and several outbuildings.

Behind the house and bordering it were woods, all encased by a stone wall. The buildings sat back from the
gravel road on a small hill, surrounded by maple trees.
The house was honey pear in color, a light yellow, with
white shutters. The house had a nice open porch with
slender white turned posts that led up to curved filigree.
The front door to the house was situated on the porch
to the right, and to the left of the front door were two
sets of side-by-side floor-to-ceiling windows.

He headed to the front door on the porch but heard
a voice coming from behind the house. As he walked
over the little hill, there was a weathered-grey horse
barn. There she was.

He stopped walking when he saw her. She was talking to her horse while petting it. He felt like he was
interrupting a private conversation. The horse gave
him away, raising its head and looking onto the drive
right at him. She turned her head in the same direction
and saw him. He resumed walking to her. As he approached her, he took her in. He roughly guessed that
she was a few years younger than he. Her hair showed
tints of blonde running through its length. He blushed
at admiring her curves. Her eyes were a faded blue, her
high cheekbones were flushed with the afternoon heat
of the sun. Her lips, her mouth unsteadied him, and he
stopped short of the barn door. When she spoke to him,
her voice was pleasant. As she asked him questions,
he responded. But now, lying on his bed, he couldn't
recall what he had said. He remembered looking at her
horse, a fine Appaloosa. She was dark grey with a white

speckled rump, her mane and tail were jet black, and she had gentle brown eyes. He loved horses. He had grown up riding them and even had an Appaloosa of his own when he was a boy in Alaska, named Soyala. He was a winter foal, and therefore was at a disadvantage in the barn with the other foals and yearlings who were bigger and stronger than he. But Soyala stood his ground and soon grew into a beautiful colt with shiny black fur and those distinctive bright white speckles on his rump.

Zander approached her Appaloosa, and after getting its approval, he petted its soft fur while stealing sideways glances at her. Her kindness of the sub was unexpected, and he found it awkward. He thanked her, then turned back to the road where the van was parked. He swung the van door closed, putting the sub beside his water bottle, and shifted into gear and headed to the next delivery. The color and the warmth in his cheeks finally subsiding.

He turned over onto his side, facing the wall, the fingers on his left hand drumming an impatient beat on his ribs. It was now 2 a.m. He sat up, putting his feet on the floor, his elbows on his legs, his head in his hands. He sighed and ran his hand through his haphazardly cut hair and raised his head with another sigh. He laced his fingers together. Beads of sweat formed on his bare chest. He rose quickly, pulling his grey sweatpants up a bit and went over to the window to look out at the usual scene, the bright lights of the streetlamps, the neon signs from the bars still glowing, the red brake lights from the cars. There would be no sleep for him. He pulled on a hoodie and slipped on sneakers, grabbing his gym bag and his keys as he went out the door.

Zander was a loner, a practice to which he was accustomed. He never really fit in anywhere. He never questioned it, never wondered if it was due to him being an only child, or having to grow up so fast, or, as he got older, if it had more to do with his stature. Walking down the street in the early hours of the morning, Zander didn't have a cautious bone or thought. He stood six-foot-two, which alone may not deter some from his figure, but his build and how he moved, and how he walked—he had a definite swagger. His hoodie was taut against his chest and arms, defining his muscles. Anyone who could catch a glimpse of his facial features between the streetlights and shadow of his hoodie saw a man with eyes that changed from blue to hazel depending on the situation. His lips were tightly pressed together, a strong jaw with scruff along the jawline, a tattoo peeking out from the opening of his hoodie going up the side of his neck, a line of a scar running through his left eyebrow down to the top of his cheekbone. To some he was attractive, to others he was too harsh; there was no in between.

Zander made his way to an undesirable part of town only a few blocks from his apartment. He was heading for a large grey, rectangular cinder-block building. The ground level boasted a basketball court, indoor tennis court, and a large boxing arena where professional matches were held. The basement level housed the gym, weights, punching bags, jump ropes, treadmills, and stationary bicycles that were positioned around the perimeter of two roped-off sparring rings. Instead of continuing straight to the main entrance of the gym, which faced one of the main streets in the city that ran its length, Zander turned into the alley behind the gym. He easily went down the four stairs to the metal-encased door to be buzzed in. He raised his head to the security camera and pulled his hoodie back a bit from his face.

Bruce the security guard knew it was Zander even without seeing his face. Bruce watched the sneakered feet on the security camera nimbly come down the cracking cement steps. Few other patrons were up this early. As the hours got closer to daylight, more members would come in before starting their workdays. The buzzer rang loud in the alleyway, and Zander pulled the door open with ease. He gave a slight nod to Bruce, who raised a finger to his forehead in a salute. In his other hand he held a magazine, at a glance it looked like a *National Geographic*. Bruce was every part the security guard, standing at six-foot-six and weighing in at 260 pounds of muscle. He used his free gym membership that came with working security at the gym to his advantage. He worked out every free moment when he wasn't reading. He had a very serious look to him; no one had ever seen him smile. And he was loyal to Mickey, the owner of the gym. He had worked there since he was nineteen. Never having the option to go to college, he absorbed books, magazines, and trivia, and was probably one of the most knowledgeable guy's Zander had ever met. When the training matches got personal, Bruce would come out of his encased room and haul the unruly out of the gym, comparing their feud to one written by Shakespeare and offering a solution written by Thomas and Kilmann, as out into the back alley the fighters would go. Zander had never been hauled out by Bruce or anyone else, he kept his fighting about fighting. But tonight, there was something in him he couldn't quite place. But when he landed his first punch on his sparring mate, he put a name to it: *Desire*.

When he made it to the showers, he was hoping for sublime exhaustion to wash over him, but instead his mind went back to her barn and the tilt of her head and when a piece of her hair fell in her eyes how she brushed it away with her hand. The steam surrounded him and began to fill up the room. Through the steam one could make out the dark ink on his left arm, a detailed mountain range was prominent on his wrist, leading to a tattoo going up his bicep that curved and split off into three prongs, one traveling around to his back, one crept over his collar bone, and the third curled up his neck, their tips looking like flames of a fire. Along his right arm, beginning at his wrist, were twisted roots of a tree. Woven into the bottommost root was a name that he had only heard whispered in his family. As the roots continued, laced into them were names from past generations of the Blake family line. The base of the tree boasted the names of his grandfather, mother, and father. Along the beginning of the tree's trunk, was Emil's name. The gnarled top branches of the tree turned into an antler, a large, impressive rack that covered his bicep, the antlers sprawling over onto his pec and upper back. On his torso, block lines were across his liver, phases of the moon ran along his rib cage, the word *Reins* on his chest was wrapped in one of the prongs that ran from his left arm and the antler coming from the right. Centered on his back he carried the mark of a single raven's wing with exquisite, detailed feathers, this was entwined in both the antler and the prong that circled to his back. Zander put the palms of his hands on the tile of the shower wall and, hanging his head, he let the water cascade down his body. He let out a sigh, the water vibrating off his lips, and then closed his eyes.

Zander was standing on the loading dock with Brad Jameson, a fellow delivery driver, for Farm & Pharma. Farm & Pharma was built singlehandedly with private investors who backed the CEO, Roberta Post. It was the first of its kind. Not only did it have a school for medical research and development, it also was a distributor of the medicines, for both animals and humans. The headquarters was situated in a centrally located city, but it had small facilities in the surrounding towns that were referred to as satellite clinics and were open from nine to five. They held some of the more common medications that might be needed to restock a hospital, a doctor's office, or a veterinarian's supply in a pinch. Another unique feature: the majority stockholder was a woman. It was rumored that Roberta Post was someone not to trifle with, that she was ruthless in her business ventures and had connections on both sides of the law.

Brad watched the loaders go from the stacks in the back to the vans at the loading docks. They went back and forth, checking labels on boxes against papers on a clipboard. Every once in a while, Brad would push some of the mop of his dark blonde hair out of his green eyes. Zander took a sip from his water bottle.

After losing interest in the loaders, Brad spoke, "Hey, thanks for swapping those days with me, Zander. Hopefully, my class schedule stays the same next semester."

"No problem," Zander mumbled.

"You seem even more quiet than usual, you okay?" Brad asked.

"Hmmm, fine," Zander mumbled. Days had passed since the time he first met her; he had hoped that his want to get to know her would disappear, her voice and image would vanish from his mind, his desire for her would fade with the passing of time. However, now he was faced with someone who knew her and could fuel this force he felt, but having never been in this situation before, Zander wasn't sure how to proceed. Luckily, Brad was chatty and easygoing, both characteristics Zander admired in him.

"I was right about the hospital, wasn't I, Jeremy the orderly? I mean it's good he's OCD, but man he takes forever counting the pills in the vials and checking the packaging is sealed on the boxes. He is super nice and great with the patients though," Brad stopped only long enough to take half a sip of his coffee and then he was off again. "Oh hey, Waverly Germaine, the vet in Easton, I delivered to her yesterday. She mentioned she met you."

Zander took another sip of water and turned to face Brad; his mind was wondering what she had said about him. Before he could decide to ask or not, Brad was off talking again.

"I told her to watch out for you, because you're a smooth talker," Brad paused, looking at Zander, and recognized the pissed-off look on his face. "I'm joking, man. I did tell her that we went to the Academy together and that you box. I also said you were pretty good at it."

Zander was now staring into the back of the van, nodding his head, all of a sudden very aware of the sleeves on his work shirt feeling too warm on his arms. He began rolling them up while Brad continued talking.

"If she seemed a bit standoffish, it's only because she doesn't know you. She was born in Easton and her family was very well respected. Her parents were doctors up in the hospital there."

Zander cut in, "Were?"

"Yeah, they both have passed on. Her father was recent. While we were at the Academy, she was sent off to school and then went on to graduate school. Her mother passed away during that time. She came back permanently when her dad got sick and set up her practice. Anyway, being alone in that house and seeing you, a stranger, especially you, man," Zander looked at Brad with a questioning look. "No offense, Zander, but you do give a hard impression. I mean your tattoos and muscles,

11

for anyone who doesn't know you, you know?" Brad was thinking he'd need a big shovel to get out of this mess, but Zander looked thoughtful as he looked down at his exposed arms covered in ink, as if seeing them for the first time and just realizing the assumptions that could be made about him. Brad continued tentatively, "anyway, now she knows who you are." To lighten the tone a bit he added, "oh, and I told her to not spoil you with those subs."

"That was unexpected," Zander replied.

"Yeah, when she first gave me one it was, but now I'm used to it." Brad said.

"How do you get used to someone's kindness?" Zander asked, looking off to nowhere.

"I don't mean like used to where I expect it or I don't appreciate it, I thank her," Brad said. "I mean more like I'm used to her; Waverly and I chat when I make a delivery. I've told her about Sonny. She's been encouraging with me going back to school. She is pretty thoughtful."

Zander remained deep in thought until the noise of the van's back doors being drawn down and locked in place, ready for their evening deliveries, pulled him back to the present.

"I'll see you later, Zander," Brad said as he headed for his van, thinking about what Zander had said. Waverly didn't have to get him those subs. He should do something nice for her to show his appreciation.

Zander turned to Brad, gave a nod of his head, and headed for the driver's side of his own van. Sliding in behind the wheel and placing the belt over his lap, he turned the keys, reached down between the seat and console for the clipboard, and logged in the beginning mileage. After checking the mirrors, he pulled out away from the loading dock and headed for his first stop.

Driving came easily for Zander. He hadn't been on the job long, and already he knew the best routes to take to make the deliveries. He was able to maneuver the van with ease along the city streets and the countryside's one-lane covered bridges. As he drove, he ruminated about the conversation he just had with Brad. She had asked about him, but Brad conveyed it was more about not knowing him than in interest. He looked down at his arms and ran his right hand along the forearm of the left, as if able to erase the dark tattoos, which were permanent. He held out his right hand. Tattoed on the knuckles of the pointer, middle, and ring were the numerals 4-5-6.

Mile after mile, delivery after delivery, Zander passed the time on his shift. He had a fight that night and appreciated the distraction the work provided. Finally, Zander pulled his van into Farm & Pharma's back loading area. He logged the mileage on the clipboard, locked up the doors, threw the keys into the afterhours lock box, and then headed home. His apartment was in a six-story brick building. There were four such identical buildings in a row, separated by narrow alleys. He turned his key in the outer door lock and pushed in. It slammed shut behind him as he pushed through a set of plexiglass doors where the mailboxes were. He didn't bother checking his—he never had mail. He ran up the stairs two at a time to his fourth-floor apartment. Once inside, he tossed his key ring on the small stand

and flicked on the overhead light. He rolled down his sleeves and unbuttoned his work shirt as he headed for the bathroom. He hit the light switch and tossed the shirt into the hamper. Running the water in the sink, he looked at himself in the mirror. Considering Brad's words, he hoped that he would make an impression on tonight's opponent. He splashed some water over his face, then changed into his warm-up clothes, grabbed his gym bag and keys, and headed out the door and down the stairs through the front doors and onto the dark street. He had sparred with this guy before, and his older brother. He had their signature moves down in his head when he pictured fighting them in the ring. He bounced down the steps to the back entrance of the gym, where he was buzzed in. Swinging the metal door open with ease, he glanced at Bruce who, through the cage, said, "I'll be out there tonight cheering you on, man."

Zander gave him a quick nod. His coach and the owner of the gym, Mickey, came to his side as Zander made his way to the locker room. His silver hair stuck out from under a tilted baseball cap he would flip off and on nervously when watching fights. His dark blue eyes never missed a foul or a missed opportunity in the ring for his trainees. "You ready for Travis tonight, kid?" Zander nodded his head, "Okay, cause we're gonna have a crowd. That toff has his brother here, too."

Zander looked toward the sparring ring, seeing Travis and his older brother, Corey. They paused from their practice momentarily and watched Zander. Zander kept moving to the locker room. Mickey had been a decent middle-weight boxer back in his day in Britain. He was known for his slight build and quick footing, using those as an advantage against his opponents. He was an even better coach. Other labels like husband, father, and grandfather he could not wear across his back, but all Zander was looking for was a coach and access to the gym and ring, all of which Mickey took care of. Retired from the ring, he found his way to the states where he had the opportunity to own the gym and boxing arena. In the locker room, Mickey continued to talk, trying to rev Zander up but also keep him in line. Zander's last fight with Travis was called. This was the rematch. Travis was faster than his brother Corey. Both were avid boxers and shorter than Zander but had wide shoulders and muscular chests that led to a narrow waist. Travis, the younger brother, still had that roundness to his facial features, whereas Corey, the older of the two, had a more defined jaw. Their dark brown hair was shaved in military style, and their eyes were also dark brown and reminded Zander of a shark's when, in the ring they appeared to be black, vacant. Travis, Corey, their father, and their uncle had all been a part of the boxing scene well before Zander had entered. They had quite the following, even had their own gym in a more up-and-coming part of the city. Due to city zoning, however, they still had to come to this side of the billboards, the *back sides* it was called, for matches. Zander had faced more difficult opponents, both inside and outside of the ring, but he listened to Mickey's advice and warnings as he changed, knowing he hadn't learned everything there was to learn.

"You want to do some punches? Some throws on the bag?"

"Hmmm . . . ," Zander replied.

"Okay, then let's go."

Mickey led Zander back out to the gym. They walked, focused on the row of gym bags hanging in a line, both well aware that Travis and Corey watched them closely. Mickey stood behind the punching bag, bracing it, while Zander began his warm-up. Mickey's accent and use of slang made it difficult to always understand him, Zander went more by his tone. He kept his eyes on the center of the bag and let Mickey's cursing wash over him. In his mind, he replayed the moves of Travis from that first fight and coordinated his responses on the bag.

His warm-up done, Mickey, the cut man—Vinnie, and Zander were back in the locker room. Mickey's curses and nicotine-stained finger were in Zander's face while Vinnie wrapped his hands. The locker room was empty except for the three of them, but it was anything but quiet. Zander just kept nodding his head, he'd heard this lecture before but took it all in.

"You're nothing here, and they want to keep it that way. They have got the crowd out there; all you got is you. Turn them, boy. You're gonna walk out them doors and those bimbos will be there, paid for by Travis to distract you. Keep your fucking eyes on the ring!"

For a split second, Zander's mind went to Waverly brushing her hair out of her eyes. Mickey immediately slapped Zander across the face. "Oy boy! Focus!"

Zander shook his head, getting her image out of his mind. Vinnie, who was wearing his lucky newsboy cap, tilted it back a bit while wrapping Zander's hand, revealing the shaved, salt-and-pepper hair of a middle-aged man. Vinnie had been working with Mickey for years now as the cut man to Mickey's trainees. Vinnie had a paunch to his gut, which he closed only two buttons of a sweater over. His dark eyes were set under bushy black eyebrows, which furrowed when watching the fights. Vinnie was done, and stood up, "Okay, son, you're wrapped."

Zander rose and jogged in place for a bit, moving his head from side to side to loosen up. He swung his arms in circles then said, "Okay."

Out of the locker room they went, and through the gym, which was empty, members were most likely out in the arena to see the fight or knew on fight nights that the gym would be closed and were elsewhere. They stood before a set of metal doors at the opposite end of the gym entrance. Mickey and Vinnie pushed them open for Zander. They walked the long, inclined hall leading to the arena. Finally, Zander stood behind the curtain hung in front of the propped-open doors. He could feel the heat and hear the noise from the crowd. He knew Mickey's words were right—he had no one, he was no one, even though he had won fight after fight. He heard the announcer call his name, and Mickey and Vinnie pulled back the curtains. Mickey was spot on—there were the ladies doused in cheap perfume, clawing at Zander with their fake nails and fake faces, trying to kiss him, distract him. Mickey and Vinnie pushed them off as Zander turned away from their advances, his sights set on the ring. As he moved closer to the ring, the air was heavy with cigar smoke. Zander made his way to his corner and Mickey and Vinnie began to set up. Zander looked at Travis. In his corner he had his coach, manager, and family. He had an entourage with him. Zander thought, *He's gonna need it.*

The referee, who everyone called Smitty, was excitable, loud, consistent, and fair with his calls. He was short in stature, his snow-white hair neatly trimmed and parted to one side. His face was ruddy in complexion, his nose was bent in such a way you could tell it had been broken a few times, his eyes—a light blue—were fast and darted around, reading the room and the people. He'd been a ref for years and had called some of the greatest fights. Travis and Corey's father had hired him for this particular fight. His personal opinion about the fighters mattered to the bookies, but for tonight's fight he kept his opinion to himself, as he was in a delicate situation with being paid for by the family of a fighter.

Smitty could size up the fighters on any given day. In his mind, he was calling the fights before they had even begun. In his free time before a fight, he'd swing by the gyms and watch them train. He knew which ones fought dirty and which ones fought fair. He knew which ones wanted to earn titles and which ones expected them to be handed to them. This fight was no different in sizing these two fighters up. One wanted to earn, the other expected. Travis was fast and quick, but overly confident. Zander had the stamina to wear Travis down. Tonight, Smitty saw something in Zander's eyes. Something he hadn't observed before, and something he hadn't considered with this one. Travis never had that look in his eyes.

The seats of the first two rows of Travis's entourage, besides his mother and father, were filled with female followers. They appeared to know their place in the pecking order. The flavor of the week sat beside his mother, and in order of favorites they filled the remaining seats. There was no serious emotion attached to any of them from Travis, they were status symbols, like his cars and jewelry—bit distractions. That's what Smitty saw in Zander's eyes, *Distraction*. He knew that if the kid couldn't clear that distraction—whatever or whomever it was—from his mind, the fight that Smitty was confident would be Zander's before they entered the ring, could now swing in Travis's favor.

The sparring partners approached one another and Smitty eyed them both closely, tuning out Travis's trash talk. Smitty held his arms out and yelled to the fighters, "Alright gents, I expect a clean, fair fight tonight. If not, don't cry sweethearts, I'll keep you in check," Smitty could tell Zander wasn't listening to Travis's mouth or to him. To pull him back to the present he yelled, "Keep your heads in the ring!" With that, Zander shook his head. Smitty saw the focus come back to the kid's eyes.

"Tap and step back, get ready to dance!"

With that, Travis and Zander hit gloves and moved away from one another. The little arm of the round bell swung into action, followed by Travis landing the first blow.

Three rounds in and Travis was wearing himself down. His footwork zigged and zagged in the ring, making Zander match it. The combination of the blows Travis was landing were quick and startling. He apparently hoped that eventually they would add up to wear and tear on his opponent and cause Zander to slip.

Zander was aware that Travis wanted to slow him by landing many little jabs in the same spot, over and over. Travis's punches were doing exactly what he wanted. Zander could tell that his right side would be hurting in the morning.

When the bell sounded the end of the round, the boxers went to their respective corners. In Travis', his father, brother, and coach saying encouraging words, while in Zander's corner, Vinnie was busy giving Zander water and Mickey was yelling at him. "What are you doing? The longer you keep him upright the more he's going to take you down, one peg at a time. Stop looking at him and damage him!"

Smitty, on the periphery, watched Travis and company. They were strategically planning his moves for the next round. His father was rubbing the boy's shoulders, the coach standing idly by while Corey told Travis what to look out for. He had been on the sidelines, not watching Travis but gathering intel on Zander and his stance. *A smart thing indeed*, thought Smitty. In the opposing corner, he caught glimpses of Zander, Mickey, and Vinnie. A different scene there—raised voices, cursing, and no words of encouragement coming from those ropes. Smitty caught Zander's eyes, which showed the same look as before the fight. His mind was not in the ring. Smitty felt the betting slip in his pocket and rethought his bet. Another thought crept in, that he was slipping. *I should've picked up on this distraction, whatever it was, in this kid.* Maybe it was time for him to throw in his ref stripes.

The fourth round clanged into action. The sparring partners began bobbing and weaving, their sight behind gloved fists. And there it came, a sucker punch from Travis catching Zander's right cheek. Smitty knew the sound, there would be a tear in the flesh, and sure enough when the fist cleared, Zander's face showed a fight punch right under his eye, a bruise already forming, a trickle of blood trailing down his cheek.

Zander had been looking over Travis's shoulder before the punch came. His eyes unfocused as the crowd behind his opponent had blurry, fuzzy edges. He wondered how she was sleeping. His right side relaxed, his gloved fist faltered, leaving a window open just long enough for Travis to raise his left and, full throttle, land a punch on Zander's face. From the force, his head turned away from the fuzzy crowd, his eyes now focused on the parallel lines of the ropes of the ring. In those few seconds, his thoughts went from calm—imagining her in bed, to anger—picturing Travis laid out on the mat. Zander turned his head to his cocky opponent's face; his mouth was running off insults. Smitty took a step back, he knew what was about to come. The sweat mixed into the open cut on Zander's cheek, causing it to sting. The swelling of his cheek started to rise. Zander didn't want to be in this ring, he wanted to be alone with his thoughts, and the fastest way to that was to lay Travis out.

Travis's overconfidence from landing that punch got in his way of recognizing the war had not been won, just a battle. Zander threw a counter punch and Travis was caught off guard, leaving his left side exposed, and Zander went for a quick combination. One punch landed on Travis's left side and the next was a right jab to under Travis's chin. Travis's body ricocheted, trying to catch up and block from left to right the gravity of Zander's punches as they kept coming and landing. Travis had become weary during the prior three rounds, and he was not prepared for the speed and energy Zander had pulled from somewhere. With the last punch landing on Travis's jaw, he staggered backward, his eyes rolling in the back of his head. Then his left leg bent under, and he was gone, floating down to the mat. Zander placed his hands at chest level waiting for the final count from Smitty pounding on the mat. The noise from the crowd was deafening. The fight was over, Zander had won. Smitty grabbed Zander's wrist and held his arm high, announcing his victory. Mickey and Vinnie rushed the mat. All Zander could think was it seemed like a long way from the ring to the quiet of his apartment. Zander turned to Mickey, "Get me out of here."

"Okay, boy. Let's move," replied Mickey.

The ropes were held up and Zander passed under, followed by Mickey and Vinnie.

Travis lay on the mat surrounded by his brother, father, coach, and medics. Smitty stood back, watching the scene. Travis sat up in a daze. Smitty turned his attention to Zander, who was leaving the ring. *He didn't waste any time getting out of the ropes,* Smitty thought. Not that he could blame him, the crowd was sour after seeing their prince fall. Smitty noticed a man step out from the rows of chairs and fall in behind the trio. He was wearing a black hoodie and black jeans and pushed through the swaying curtains after Zander.

Zander made his way down the incline to the metal doors of the gym. He could listen to Mickey and Vinnie in the locker room, and he could start to unwind in the shower. But he heard someone calling his name from behind. It was a voice he recognized but couldn't place, and he slowed. Mickey turned and looked at the owner of the voice following behind them. "He don't talk with anyone," Mickey said as he held up his hands, trying to dissuade the guy.

"Hey Zander, you remember me?" the guy asked. Zander turned. Kit Mayfield. They had gone to school at the Academy together. Kit's face was pale and had a sheen to it. Even though it was warm in the arena, he wore a long-sleeve black hoodie. His shaggy black hair looked greasy. Holding up his black jeans, which were

27

two sizes too large, was a large oval silver belt buckle with the Mayfield insignia on it.

Zander nodded, staring right into his eyes. Zander remembered him exactly for who he was: a rich man's son with rage problems, and by the look of him those weren't the only problems.

Kit wanted to make it clear to the three men who he was. "Kit, Kit Mayfield. Great fight out there tonight."

One to get straight to the point, Zander squared off to Kit. "What do you want?"

"Nothing, man, just wanted to say hi, let you know I was here. See if you wanted to go for a drink."

"No, I don't think so. You take care of yourself, Kit," Zander turned his back to him, and Mickey and Vinnie followed suit.

Kit, offended that this nobody would dare turn their back to him, reached out to grab Zander's arm when Mickey stepped in. "Whoa, you're gonna want to watch where you put your hands there, mate."

"I'm not your fucking 'mate'," Kit snapped back at Mickey.

Zander turned and raised his hands. "Hey, there's no need for that. Slow down there, Kit, before you find yourself back out there," with his head Zander motioned to the arena.

Kit stepped back and ran his hands through his hair. "Yeah, okay, whatever." He turned, muttering something under his breath.

Mickey went to take a step forward, but Zander caught him and shook his head. The three of them continued to the locker room. Once inside the grey cement walls lined with galvanized metal lockers, Mickey and Vinnie recapped the fight with what they saw, what they wanted to see, and what Zander needed to be aware of for the next time as far as his moves went and the next time, he would face Travis or Corey.

Zander cut in, "Do you two know who that guy was?"

"He said his name, I don't remember it," Vinnie said.

"I didn't catch it either," said Mickey.

"That was Harold Mayfield's son," Zander stated.

"Really? What would the likes of him be doing here?" asked Vinnie.

"He's been slumming it for a while now here in the city," said Mickey, "or so I've heard. Scoring over on the bridge and staying in the bricks."

The bridge and bricks were slang for those who knew the city well. The bridge was an old, no longer in use train trestle where drugs and sex were for sale and other unseemly business was conducted. The bricks were old mills not far from the bridge, also no longer in use, where some homeless bunkered down, but mostly for those whose addictions had cast them out of the homes of families and friends. It gave them cover and a place to get high.

It was Zander's turn to lecture them. He grabbed his towel, "The name Mayfield is familiar to you both, and you know the weight behind it. So next time, Mickey, you're looking to start something, know who it is you're facing and who has their back," Zander said. "Oh," he continued, "if you see him before I do in the arena again, let me know."

Zander made his way into a shower stall and turned on the showerhead, letting the stall fill with steam as he undressed. Seeing Kit had unnerved him.

After much consideration and discussion with the elders, Emil decided to send Zander away. Sent him away from the last place he had been with his family. The last place he had seen his grandfather, father, and mother alive. Emil had taken him in, there was no place else for him to go, no other family to speak of. Emil Attla was the son of an elder with the Athabaskan people. He was a guide to hunters and prospectors, and it was said that the land flowed through him, that he was so engrained in it that it wasn't possible to tell where one began and one ended. The Pipe and Oil Company and the borough selected him to survey the land, along with the professional grade surveyors, to decide the best placement of the Trans Alaskan Pipeline. He took the work and the concerns of his people seriously. When he met Zander's grandfather, Geoffrey Blake, before agreeing to work with the man they first had to share stories of their lives. Emil was impressed that this man from one of the Lower 48's was much like him. He came from a long line of explorers and navigators; it was in his blood. Geoffrey was a remarkable figure of a man. His posture was straight, which made him a towering figure. His silver hair was tucked into an old sea captain's hat that had been handed down to him. He had a full beard, which he kept trimmed, and in his later years he wore gold-rimmed glasses that accentuated his blue-hazel eyes. He was a handsome man who had married the love of his life. When she passed, leaving him a son, he raised Jacob the best he could.

While Geoffrey Blake continued to build the family fortune, Jacob had gone to school for engineering, where he met Klara, who was studying to be an environmental conservationist, her work focused primarily on the migratory patterns of animals. The couple married while in their junior year of college. They were a handsome couple. Klara with her long, dark, chestnut hair and large, expressive brown eyes, her curves that loved to be on the dance floor, and Jacob with his light brown hair and blue eyes like his mother. His build was trim from being on the rowing team. People who met them were taken in by their kind features and the way the couple made everyone feel at ease.

When the opportunity came knocking for Geoffrey to survey the land for TAPS, he convinced his son it would be the adventure of a lifetime, one that may never happen again. The family pulled up stakes and moved out to the wilderness of Alaska. As a young boy, Zander couldn't wait for the chance to help alongside both his parents and his grandfather. Emil took to the family as they did to him, along with the different cultures that they were now surrounded with. Carefully the land was surveyed in all seasons and in some of the harshest conditions. Emil, Geoffrey, and Jacob pressed on to meet deadline after deadline, facing blizzards, wolves, and the objectors, those against the pipe and who did not think twice about taking another's life when standing up for what they believed in.

As the years passed and the pipe took form over the Alaskan landscape, Zander also grew and took form. He was growing up in what he thought was the best of both worlds. He went to school, but then he went with Emil to visit the elders regularly and absorbed all he could. He learned how to ride horses and he learned how to connect with the land by learning from the Native Alaskans. He listened to the stories they told, and he listened to the wind moving over the untamed tundra.

Being sent away was a punishment for Zander. "I should stay here with you. Why did you take me in just to send me away? Emil, you gave me a name," Zander pleaded.

Emil took Zander's shoulders in his hands and spoke firmly, "You are Zander Blake—"

Zander cut in, "I'm Zander Reins!"

Emil grabbed his shoulders, "No, you are Zander Blake, son of Jacob and Klara, grandson of Geoffrey. You must leave here and become your own man."

Emil spun Zander to face the oncoming train. After he boarded the train, Zander purposefully sat on the side where he could not see Emil and Quinn, who waited on the platform to see him off.

Emil turned to Quinn. "How can I just let the boy go?"

"He wasn't ours to begin with. He needs to go out and find his way, not my way, not your way, not our way, but his way," responded Quinn.

"I don't know if I should let him go."

Quinn put his weathered hand on Emil's shoulder. "If he comes back to us, it will be part of his story then," Quinn responded with a heavy heart.

Zander turned in the shower, tipping his head back and letting the water wash over him. He remembered navigating the way through train stations, watching the countryside through one windowpane at a time. He arrived at his destination just in time for the Academy's fall semester to begin. He stood in the doorway to the Admissions building of Gyrfalcon Academy for boys. He pulled out the envelope that Emil had given him with instructions to give it to the headmaster and all would be taken care of. The Academy, with its brick exterior and white Grecian pillars with white trim and gold dome on the roof, looked to Zander to be more of a capital building than a school. Zander's knock on the door echoed through the quiet halls of the Admissions building. It was such a harsh rap that Natalie Thayer dropped the stack of books she was carrying. She was just finishing up a few things the night before the rush of the fall term. Over the next few days, teachers, students, and parents were due to arrive. She picked up the books and put them on a side table in the hall, then went to the front door, wondering who could possibly be knocking. The knock caused Rupert Thayer, Natalie's husband, and the headmaster of the Academy, to go down the flight of stairs to the front hall where Natalie was. He, too, wondered who would be knocking at this hour. He joined Natalie as she opened the door. There stood a young man on the doorstep, with a suitcase in one hand and an envelope that he held out to the Thayer's in the other. Rupert reached forward and took the envelope while Natalie greeted the boy. The look on his face stung her heart. He looked very lost.

She ushered him inside. "Well, hello, young man. Come in, come in. I'm Mrs. Thayer and this is Head-master Thayer. What is your name?"

"Zander Reins," he replied, then said, "no, sorry Blake, Zander Blake."

"Well, alright then," replied Natalie hesitantly, but decided against asking him about the discrepancy. Rupert meanwhile read the note in the envelope the boy held out and looked at the check that was also enclosed.

"Oh yes, we received word from your guardian to add you to this year's roster." The boy just stared at the floor. After a pause, Rupert continued, "Well, let's get you settled in then. You'll be alone tonight, but the rest of the boys will start arriving in the morning." Rupert put the envelope in his inside jacket pocket and was about to lead the boy out the door and to the dormitory.

Natalie broke in, "You must be hungry after your travels. Why don't you come up to the house and I'll make you some supper?"

Rupert agreed, "Yes, wonderful idea, I could do with a bit of supper myself." He turned the key to lock the main door and the three of them set out across the quad toward a charming white house with gingerbread trim and a porch swing.

Zander remained quiet throughout the meal and provided short answers; by all rights he was an orphan. The Thayer's had been renovating the headmaster's house and, at present, the guestrooms were all in one stage of renovation or another. Natalie insisted Zander stay with them that night on a makeshift bed for the boy on the blue velvet sofa in the living room.

"We will be right upstairs if you need anything. Try to get some sleep. In the morning, Mr. Thayer will take you to the dormitory to choose your room and get you settled. There will be some paperwork to complete, and then we'll get a teacher to test you for grade level. Sweet dreams, Zander," Natalie said, pulling the pocket doors toward one another, leaving a bit of space. Zander lay on the made-up couch and bent his legs to better fit on the sofa.

Natalie turned away from the doors. She went over to the late summer roses that were arranged in a silver vase on the entryway table. Her mind was roaming. *What an interesting young man, well boy as he was fourteen, but so much like a young man.* He stood almost as tall as Rupert. He carried himself with confidence, he had taken the jar of olives right out of Natalie's hand and twisted the lid as if it were nothing. Then there were the tattoos. Natalie had never seen tattoos like that on anyone that age before. Numbers on his knuckles, and she had caught a glimpse of a mark on his neck leading down his arm when he pulled on his t-shirt to sleep in. He was so quiet. She twisted the vase a few times, settling on its placement, and then headed for the stairs. *What an interesting boy indeed*, she thought and then thought of his name, *Zander Reins, no wait, Zander Blake*. It sounded so familiar, but she couldn't place it.

She was going up the stairs, passing by photos she'd recently hung of her and Rupert, along with some photos of the Germaine's, their best friends in Easton. When she got to the little landing, she was greeted by her multi-colored cat, Scrabble. Natalie stooped to pick the friendly feline up. Upon rising, Natalie's eyes lingered on the gold nameplate attached to an elaborate frame that held a handsome oil painting of one of the founders of Easton. This painting, as was tradition, was to hang in the headmaster's house. The picture was of a retired sea captain, an explorer in his days, back when there were still places on a map that were unknown.

Staring back at Natalie was a name, Ezekiel Blake. Natalie, petting Scrabble, whispered to her, "We must tell Rupert, perhaps there is a connection to Zander." Natalie carried Scrabble into the bedroom. Rupert was fast asleep, no doubt worn out due to the tizzy of the expectant teachers, students, and parents, as well as all the preparations leading up to the new school year. She, too, was tired and readied herself for bed. *First thing in the morning* she thought, while turning out the light on her bedside stand, *first thing in the morning I'll tell Rupert about the name on the painting.*

Meanwhile Scrabble, knowing a new person was in the house and curious, decided to investigate and headed down the stairs, taking a left into the little space open between the pocket doors. There Zander was, laying on his back, looking toward the window seat and out into the night. Scrabble made her way over and leaped up onto him. He reached down, removing one hand from behind his head, and began to pet her. She settled in between Zander and the back of the sofa, purring intensely, the tip of her tail flicking contentedly.

The next morning was a hectic one, not just for the Thayer's but for all of the staff at the Academy. Cars filled the long, tree-lined drive leading up to the Admissions building. There another line formed of students and parents waiting to be greeted with paperwork for the trusted Academy to take charge of their most precious possessions. With the hustle and bustle of the morning and with the new charge of looking after Zander, Natalie forgot to tell Rupert about the painting and the name, it was forgotten for the time. Zander, bathed and dressed, sat patiently with Scrabble on the sofa when Natalie came in, opening the pocket doors. She was smiling at him.

"Alright, Zander, let's get you and Scrabble some breakfast and head on up to the Admissions office. I'll help fill out the paperwork for you and then Rupert will take you to the dorms." Her hand fell on his back as he passed her, heading to the kitchen where he smelled the pleasant smell of oatmeal and toast. He hadn't had much physical contact with others since his parents died, and he felt himself relax with her touch.

In the kitchen, Zander watched the Thayer's move about as if choreographed. When one went to the cupboard, the other went to the fridge, and then they would meet in the middle, one with a glass the other with a bottle of orange juice. Mr. Thayer, with his ironed shirt and crooked tie, caught sight with his dark brown eyes the twisted collar on Mrs. Thayer's blouse and lifted her dark hair from her necklace. Meanwhile Mrs. Thayer, spying with her light brown eyes the crooked tie, straightened it under Rupert's chin. Zander remembered his parent's doing a similar routine in the morning; it spoke to a couple who were in sync with one another.

In the Admissions office, Natalie left Zander and his completed forms with Ms. Turner, whose cursive script filled out the remainder of the clerical information on Zander's paperwork and attached it all to a new crisp file folder. Zander's processing was easy as there wasn't much to fill in, no parents or siblings. For any mail, he gave an address of a General Store that also acted as the Post Office. Ms. Turner came around her desk carrying her camera.

"Alright now Zander, stand tall against the wall and I'll take your picture for the files."

Zander moved to the wall where there was a measuring guide painted on it with black paint. He lined himself up.

Ms. Turner was used to bending over some to get the boys in the shot, now she corrected her posture and stood up, saying, "Well you are tall for your age."

Flash, the camera made a clicking noise and Ms. Turner pushed the lever on the side with her thumb to move the film along to be ready for the next boy. Rupert was called over from his office to bring Zander to the uniform allotment room. There he was to meet Mr. Luchino Sergio, who was not only the keeper of the uniforms but was also the tailor in Easton. When Zander walked through the door, Mr. Sergio couldn't stop his jaw from dropping, but quickly recovered.

"Mr. Sergio, this is Zander, he's new to the Academy and will need all the allotments," Rupert said, introducing the two.

"Ah but of course, come here my boy, let's get some measurements." Mr. Sergio hung out his measuring tape and expertly calculated lengths and waistline, then he gathered Zander's shoe size. Once Zander had been sized up, Mr. Sergio turned and walked past rows of shelves along the room walls to where the larger sizes were.

"Looks like I'll have to pull from the senior boys' clothing area," Mr. Sergio mumbled, "Not a problem!" he quickly exclaimed.

Crisp white t-shirts, crisp white oxfords, several pairs of black socks, and three blue-and-grey striped ties were all pulled from their respective locations.

"The grey wool pants are for winter, you will find you will need them here," Mr. Sergio said.

Rupert added, "Zander's from Alaska. I'm thinking our winters will be mild compared to what he's used to."

Mr. Sergio tilted his head down and looked over his eyeglasses at Zander. He turned back to the stacks of clothing on the shelves. "The blue pants are for Fall and Spring," he added them to the pile he had started on the large wooden table in the middle of the room.

He grabbed a pair of shoes and a pair of sturdy winter boots in Zander's size from shoe racks and placed them neatly to the side of the clothing pile on the table. He then went over to the opposite wall where two bars hung, one on top of the other. Hanging from them were the blazers, each with a gold crest on the front pocket—the crest of Gyrfalcon Academy. They were arranged left to right, smallest to largest. Mr. Sergio pulled down two from the right side and placed them on the table. From a card catalogue he removed a blank uniform allotment card and began to write the items laid out on the table on the card in neat print.

"Mr. Thayer, the total comes to—," Mr. Sergio began.

Rupert cut in. "It's all taken care of, Mr. Sergio."

Mr. Sergio looked up briefly at Rupert, having had this conversation before. Many boys were simply dropped off at the front door by their parents in shiny cars, their keep paid for in advance. Mr. Sergio was tactful and continued, "Well then Master Zander, I just need you to sign your card, then I'll give you a receipt," Mr. Sergio placed all of Zander's allotment into a duffel bag, much like the one a soldier would use, made from the same sturdy green canvas.

Zander stepped forward, took the pen in his hand, and signed the receipt, *Zander Reins*. Mr. Thayer, seeing this, leaned over, and asked "Reins?" Zander crossed it out and signed *Blake* next to it.

The dormitories were built in the same fashion as the Admissions building, brick with white trim. The four original dorms, one for each grade, were situated along the wood line of the property. Additional brick dorm buildings had been added when the Academy expanded their student population. Rupert was walking with Zander toward one of the original brick structures. Zander held his suitcase in one hand and the duffel bag with his new belongings in the other. Rupert asked him if he could carry anything for him, but Zander just shook his head. So, the two of them walked across the quad toward Zander's new home.

Zander wasn't used to the standardized testing and his focus wasn't on the paper before him with all the little circles to fill in for the answers. His scores put him in a lower grade. School for many can be an unsettling time and for Zander, who was literally alone in the world, it could be tougher. He was the new kid, unknown, and he was put into a class below him. Those two factors for any child could lead to taunting from others. Zander's saving grace was his appearance. He towered over his classmates as well as some of the teachers, and the expression of his facial features reflected intimidation. For those who caught a glimpse of him changing, to see the tattoos along his side, the one that ran from his bicep up a bit on his neck, or saw his hands write with his knuckles marked in ink, the taunting did not happen, but neither did the much-needed friendships. Except one student. Brad Jameson was his name. He lived locally in the next town over. He approached Zander in a carefree, easy manner. "Hi, I'm Brad," he said.

"Zander."

"So, you're new here?" Brad asked.

"Hmmmm," Zander replied.

"I live in Weston," Brad offered, "it's just the next town over. I'm going to sign up for soccer, the coach is in the gym waiting. So, are you coming?"

Zander looked at Brad, who was leaning on the doorframe to Zander's room, then looked around his sparse bedroom. All of his clothes were hanging, his shoes polished. He had nothing else to do. He turned back to Brad, "Sure."

"Cool," Brad said, pushing off of the doorframe, moving back a bit so Zander could get into the hallway. Another boy walked by, deliberately hitting Brad with his shoulder. He was thin and lanky with straight black hair. Brad watched the kid turn his head just enough to say, "Watch out, charity case."

"Oh, hey Kit," Brad replied rubbing his shoulder where he'd just been hit.

Zander looked down the hall at the kid named Kit who just kept walking. Brad spoke, "Kit Mayfield. He's kinda a big deal, well his family is. They have a ton of money. Anyone who doesn't have money, like my family, we're called charity cases because we had to get scholarships."

Zander shut the door to his room, putting his hands in his pockets, and walking steadily down the hall. "Does it matter how you got here? You're here, aren't you?" Zander posed the questions to Brad, who put his hands in his pockets like Zander and watched his walk, one he thought fit for a movie screen featuring a hero. The boys went down the stairs heading for the gym with Brad talking away about everything and anything to entertain his new friend, who strode silently by his side.

Zander turned the shower off. *Kit hasn't changed one damn bit. He was still that punk with a chip on his shoulder, pushing his way through life*, he thought. The last time he had seen him was a couple months ago at a fight, that night Zander had gone out with Mickey and Vinnie for a drink and Kit had slid up to the bar with them. Zander wrapped his towel around his waist and cleared the fog from the mirror. He turned his head to the side, looking at the scar that ran from his left eyebrow to his cheek. And when whoever got pushed didn't move out of Kit's way, he forced them.

A group of them were in the lounge area, some were playing video games in front of the shared TV. A pair leaned on the bookcase talking about girls. Zander was tipped back in a chair, reading, his right foot on the rung of another chair to steady himself. Brad and Kit were sitting opposite one another, a chessboard with a few standing pieces between them. Zander heard Brad triumphantly say, "Checkmate!" The atmosphere changed immediately. The two playing the video game turned their heads from their entertainment, their virtual lives ended on the screen, and the guys talking gals abruptly stopped talking. Zander let his chair's legs drop. Kit stood, and the chessboard and pieces went flying through the air, landing on the common room floor. The wooden chair he had been sitting in was swung into his hands and into the air. Zander quickly, with two gliding steps, put himself into the space between Kit and Brad, who was frozen in his seat. The chair landed firmly across Zander's back, shattering to pieces. The bit that remained in Kit's hand was used to strike Zander. Kit was spewing forth a line of obscenities some of the boys had never been exposed to before as he swung the leg of the chair from over his head and cracked it on Zander's face. Zander felt his skin rip open; he felt the warm wet of his blood trickle down his head into his left eye, which he could no longer see out of and wasn't sure if it was still in his head. When Kit went to make a third strike on Zander, he raised his arm, caught the remaining chair piece, and easily twisted it out of Kit's hands. Zander now stood straight, blood soaking the left side of his face and covering his eye, the right eye stared at Kit with determination. It was a frightening sight. Kit faced him, confident he was about to have someone challenge him. The dorm aide, an adult who had been standing in the doorway after hearing the chess pieces hit the floor failed to step in, recognizing Kit and knowing too well how the situation would play out no matter who was the one to blame. When the tide turned, with Zander holding the chair leg, then and only then did the dorm aide step forward. Zander held the chair leg out to the dorm aide and walked out of the room, heading to the nurse's station.

Zander moved away from the mirror to the lockers and began to get dressed. Mickey and Vinnie were out in the gym now. Zander didn't want to see Kit ever again, wherever he went no good came of it. Zander pulled on his hoodie and zipped it up. He knew the guys would want to go out for a drink and revel in the win, but all he wanted to do was go home and sleep. He flipped the hood of his hoodie up over his head and slammed his locker shut. He went out for one beer and a shot with the boys. He sat on the barstool in one of their usual watering holes, listening to the guys talk about the fight. Finally, Zander headed home to get whatever sleep he could before work. The cool air of the night cleared Zander's mind of Kit, the days at the Academy, and, to some extent, her. Zander went up the stairs to his apartment, his hands in his hoodie pockets. The building was quiet, but in a few hours people with kids would be waking up to get them ready for school, people who worked daytime hours would be buzzing around their apartments, stirring to get coffee, breakfast, and a suitable outfit together before heading off. Zander would be well into sleep by that time. He turned the key in the lock and slid quietly into his dark apartment. He leaned on the door to push it close and swiped the hood off his head with his hand. The glow from the red brake lights from the cars below illuminated the ceiling, making the room red. He closed his eyes. The ceiling of his bedroom in his family's house in Alaska had been similarly lit, casting a hazy red glow from the fire that had consumed the house, his grandfather, and killed his mother.

A few days before Zander's father was to go out on a leg on the pipe, Zander was reading at the kitchen table and heard his father talking with some men in the front yard. The talking soon turned to the men yelling, and Zander peered out the window and saw three men with his father. He recognized them from the meetings that were held in the borough's hall, meetings designed for the people to express in an open forum their thoughts on the pipeline. But to Zander the meetings never seemed to function the way they should and often ended with the same type of men who were outside with Zander's dad yelling over one another. Zander got a good look at the men, particularly one who was pointing at his father's back as he headed for the front door away from the men. The other two were getting into a pickup truck. The man pointing his finger was yelling, "You're all gonna die for this."

Zander's mother pulled him away from the window. She then went to the front door with his father and grandfather where they spoke in hushed tones. A few days later, Zander's father hadn't checked in while out on the pipe. After the incident on the front lawn with the men, Geoffrey had taken to sleeping in the guestroom at his son's house. Klara, not able to sleep without hearing from Jacob, had taken a sleeping pill. Zander, drifting in and out of sleep, noticed a sort of brightness on his eyelids as he rolled over onto his back. He opened his eyes. His ceiling was reflecting a warm red and there was a cracking sound, like when he'd sit around the fire with Emil. He got up out of bed and went to the window. The flames were rising, curling the wood siding of the house. He ran to the hallway, which was engulfed in flames. He dodged through the hall to his parent's room. He called out for his mother, but there was no response. The noise created by the fire raged on around him. Instinctively he reached for the doorknob and felt the heat on his hand. He put his t-shirt around his hand and turned the knob. Flames and smoke were everywhere, along with the smell of something that didn't belong. One of their bedroom windows had been left open to let fresh air in. Below the window on the floor was where the odor was the strongest. There on the floor was shattered green glass. Zander saw the body of his mother. He went to her, covering his mouth with his arm, and tried to wake her, yelling at her. He wrapped her in a sheet, and dragged her through the door. He didn't remember getting through the back door, he didn't remember how he got to the front yard.

Patuk and Dika were finishing up the inventory at the General Store and Post Office; they had worked well into the night. Heading for home, Patuk turned to the sky heading out of town and to the mountains. He saw the tinge of red and smelled the smoke on the breeze. Patuk and Dika got into their truck and headed up the mountain. Behind them, a trail of trucks followed in a convoy. Blazing out of a side road in front of them they saw the headlights coming. Without slowing their truck, the other one joined and took the lead. It was Emil.

The house was completely enveloped by flames when the convoy of helpers pulled into the yard. Dika gasped as she saw Zander there in the yard, sitting next to a lump in a sheet. Emil went to Zander with Dika following with a blanket from the truck. Emil and Dika recognized the charred body of Klara, and knew she was dead. Emil pulled Zander away from his mother's body and looked the boy in the eyes.

"Where's your grandfather?" he asked Zander.

"I don't know," the boy replied.

Emil took off, joining the other helpers, and together some went into the house in search of Geoffrey. Dika wrapped the blanket around Zander and led him to the pickup truck parked in the yard. She flipped the tailgate down and Zander sat on it. She then went into the cab side of the truck and retrieved another blanket to cover Klara's body with. After doing so, she returned to Zander as she saw bright flashing lights coming up the pipe road. Zander just sat with Dika, staring at the wooden sign: Mile marker 456.

Zander pushed off the door and headed to his bed. He pulled the hoodie over his head and flung it over the bedpost and himself onto the mattress. He faced the wall, succumbing to sleep.

Zander stood on the loading dock sipping his coffee. He faced the back of the vans and watched the loaders scurrying to get the orders ready. Dusk was settling in, and the evening air was cool. Brad got out of his car carrying a white sandwich bag and a coffee cup. He made his way to Zander on the loading dock.

"I brought two muffins. Sonny outdid herself this time."

Zander looked into the bag; two plump blueberry muffins were there. He reached in and gladly took one. "Thanks," he said holding it up in a toast.

Between chewing mouthfuls Brad asked, "How'd last night go?"

"Good, he needs to protect his chin and not lead with it."

"Man, how many is that now? You've got to be up there with wins."

Zander swallowed some muffin and coffee and turned to Brad. "You'll never guess who was there last night."

Brad responded, "Waverly?"

Zander swallowed hard; he hadn't thought of her going to one of his fights as a possibility. He replied coolly, "No, why would she be there?"

"You're right. Let me think, how about—"

Zander cut in, "It was Kit Mayfield."

"You're kidding? That guy just pops up all over the place. Didn't you and he a few months ago go hang out or something?"

"No. He showed up at the bar after a fight."

"Oh," Brad said thinking about this. "Well, what was he doing there last night?"

Zander shrugged his shoulders.

Brad continued, "Well, maybe if he's up to being seen in public he'll head home to see good ole dad. Every time I drive by Mayfield's Estate, I can't help but think what a waste, man. Kit had it all and still could if he cleaned up. Did he talk to you?" asked Brad.

"He asked if I wanted to go for a drink," Zander replied flatly.

"Are you serious?"

Zander opened his mouth to answer, but Brad was off again. "After all the shit he did to you in school? What world is he living in? Who does he think he is?"

Zander slid in, "Oh he knows exactly who he is, that's the problem. And so does everyone else."

Brad turned and looked at Zander, nodding his head in agreement. The door to Brad's van slid shut as the loader locked it up and handed the invoices on the clipboard to him.

"Well, I'd better get going. I'll see you later," Brad said, jumping down from the loading dock.

Zander called after him, "Thanks again," waving the remaining bit of muffin before popping it into his mouth.

Brad gave a wave, got into his van, and headed off on his route. Zander continued to sip his coffee. He was contemplating what he would say if it had been Waverly last night at the fight instead of Kit. The clang of the van's door being locked in place brought Zander out of his thoughts. His van was packed and ready. He drained his cup and threw it into the open dumpster. He looked at his roster and flipped through the top pages. He'd be out on the road for a while tonight.

Zander walked through the door to his apartment. He was carrying his gym bag and a plastic bag from the deli a few blocks over containing his dinner. He'd had a good workout at the gym and had his night planned. A sub from the deli and the unfinished book flipped face-down on the table. He threw his keys on the stand. His laundry needed to be done. He pulled together his clothes, towels, and bedding and went down to the basement to the laundry room. A few machines were in various stages of washing and drying other tenant's clothes. Zander emptied the contents of his laundry bag into the washer and poured in some detergent. He spun the setting button, then headed back to the stairwell and up to his apartment. The red light on the answering machine immediately caught his eye. It was blinking an urgent red. He stood in front of the machine looking down at the blinking light. He reached out and pushed the button. A man's voice echoed off the apartment walls. Zander was on call for the service to make emergency deliveries, and he was needed. Zander went to his dresser and pulled out a fresh work shirt and jeans. He grabbed the plastic bag from the deli and headed out of his apartment. His brisk walk turned into a run when the rain began to fall. Ahead of him, he saw the glass and concrete building of Farm & Pharma and went down the side alley to the loading dock. The area was empty, the van already loaded. He twisted the key from his key ring into the lock box that held the keys to the vans. It was next to the afterhours lock box for returning the van keys. He took the keys for the van and unlocked the driver's side door. He saw the clipboard and slid in, moving the clipboard out of the way. He started up the van and made a mental note of the mileage while cranking up the heat to get the dampness out of the van and off his skin. He sat there for a moment, letting the air warm up. The rain making a blurry veil on the windshield, but he could make out the other white delivery vans in the enclosed area. He took out his sandwich and took a few bites, and then drank some water from his bottle. The air was warming up.

He flipped over the clipboard, taking another bite of his sandwich. Her name was at the top of the delivery sheet. He stopped chewing and felt a warm flush go over him. Slowly he turned on the headlights, shifted the van into gear, turned on the windshield wipers, and headed out onto the city streets.

What is it about rain that makes people forget how to drive? Zander was stuck in traffic on the highway. It was rush hour, and even with the rain there was no accounting for their lack of driving skills. Zander needed to get just half a mile more in his lane and he could take the exit leading out of the city and toward the country. Finally, he cleared the traffic and merged onto the ramp. The rain was heavy and fast, the van's wipers were at their highest speed, but visibility was still poor. He pulled over to the shoulder before a covered bridge to let a truck go through. While waiting for the truck to pass, he looked down at the water in the river coursing under the bridge. It was high and moving fast. The truck passed, and Zander pulled back onto the road and through the one-lane covered bridge. There he was faced with a fork in the road. A white post held two signs, their black lettering pointing in opposite directions, one for the town of Weston and one for the town of Easton. Zander went to put on his directional light but saw the river had spilled out of its banks and was in the road. Not sure how deep the water was, he took the opposite turn heading away from his destination. He'd have to take the next road heading in the direction of Easton. Unfortunately, the next available road was closed off, a crew was setting up a sawhorse with flashing lights. Zander pulled up to one of the workers and rolled the window down.

"Hey," Zander said.

The man ran to Zander, sheets of rain washing over him. "Hello! Where you trying to get to?"

"Easton way," Zander called back.

"You'll need to go three more turns south and then that road on the left, Hawk Hill, take that one. It's still open and will get you in the right direction. You know where you're going?"

"Yeah," Zander nodded. "Thank you!"

He rolled up the window and headed off in the direction the man had pointed. Zander wasn't too worried about getting lost. While spending summers at the Academy, he rode one of the Academy's bicycles around the town of Easton and most of the other dirt roads on the boundary between Easton and Weston. Zander took the turn on Hawk Hill Road and went up over a little crest. The rain continued to pour down; daylight was fading. This time he approached Waverly Germaine's home from the opposite direction. Seeing the stone walls, he slowed down. Finally, he put the van in park and looked out the window toward where the house sat on a little hill. He couldn't see or make out anything through the downpour. He gripped the steering wheel and felt his heart flutter. He pushed off the seat and slid open the door separating the driving area from the deliveries in the back. He ducked in and grabbed the box labeled with her name. He opened the side door. He still couldn't make out the house. He put the flashers on. His own thoughts were telling him the same, *Caution, slow down.* He took another breath.

As if on cue, the rain began to lighten up. The water ran along the side of the road, creating a small stream. Zander held the box of medication for her order and jumped over the water. He made his way over the little hill of her driveway. He saw the back of her pickup truck parked by the barn. The house was dark, but he made his way up onto the porch. He slowed down on the steps, not because his heart felt like it was going to explode out of his chest but because he thought he heard something. He looked at the front door. The screen door was in place, but behind it the front door was open. He stood in front of the screen door and was about to call out her name when he heard a crashing sound of something breaking. He dropped the box on the porch, and, without hesitating, he opened the screen door, heading blindly to where he heard a commotion in the back of the house. He heard a man's familiar voice, yelling something over and over, and heard the sound of something or someone being hit. With the remaining light of the day, Zander could see the man in the kitchen. He recognized Kit. Zander rounded the kitchen island and saw balled up on the floor a form he guessed was Waverly. Zander dragged Kit, his arms flailing, away from her. Zander spun him away and went to check Waverly, but Kit came at him, grabbing a knife from the countertop and began swinging it at Zander. Zander turned just in time, caught Kit's wrist, walked him backward and over to the other side of the island, and pushed him away again. This time, however,

Zander remained facing Kit. He looked at Zander and, with a smirk, lunged at him again.

Zander blocked Kit's hand that held the knife, and with his other fist landed a punch on Kit's chin. Zander's punch hardly slowed Kit down and he came at Zander again. Zander caught the look in Kit's eyes. He was high on something. Zander's only option was to take him to the floor. When Kit lunged again, Zander hooked an arm around his waist and slipped a foot behind his leg, twisting. Kit, off balance, fell backward, pulling Zander down as well. Both now on the floor, Kit still throwing punches, Zander's mind went to the curled-up ball on the other side of the island. He hadn't seen her or heard anything from that side and feared the worst. Zander landed punch after punch on Kit's face. He felt the jagged edges of Kit's teeth cut into his knuckles. He felt the wetness of Kit's blood drag across his fist from his now-busted lips. He heard the crack of an orbital bone, and then the repeated thud of flesh.

Kit reached up and grabbed Zander's shirt, tearing it. Buttons hit the floor, followed by some of Kit's teeth. He saw a shadow out of the corner of his eye run past him. He got up from Kit and followed her. She had almost made it to the door when he grabbed her arm. He wanted to see her, he had to make sure she was alright. She turned, and the gleam from the blade caught Zander's attention. It was followed by sharp pain in his left side. She had turned to face him for only a moment, and he had let go of her arm. He saw her eyes, her mouth, and the swelling on her cheek. She was no longer facing him, she had turned to the entryway table and was grabbing something, but then she hesitated. Zander pulled his hand away from his side and saw blood staining his shirt. He bent down and picked up the knife.

Zander's hand was shaking as he held the knife. He winced as he straightened himself up. The cut in his side spewed forth more blood. Zander felt with his finger, his flesh no longer intact. Instead, on his left side there was an opening. He was immediately aware of his organs on that side—intestines, stomach, kidney. He tried not to think about his insides seeping through the cut to the outside. He put his hand back over the cut. This pain was different to Zander. He looked down at the hand holding his side. The tattoos on his hand and knuckles were indecipherable, covered in blood.

Tattoo needles he was familiar with. He had ink under his skin all over. His very first marks were those he had given himself, as was his right when he had come of age. Emil had shown him and educated him on the natural inks. Zander had chosen one of the most difficult places on his skin, the knuckles on both of his hands. He would need to be steady with both his dominant and non-dominant hands. He would need to be patient. He would need to be focused. These qualities Emil had instilled in Zander, knowing he would need them throughout his life, which had already had a rough start. It was then that Emil had given Zander his name, Reins. Zander, steady and focused, envisioned the numbers on his left hand—the ring, middle, and index fingers—and he began to punch the rod with the ink and tap it with the stone. Bit by bit the numbers began to take shape. There were a few days of healing before Zander began using his non-dominant hand and began to tattoo the envisioned numbers on his knuckles. He worked with determination and knew when to stop and not continue to exhaustion. Once done, proudly on the healing knuckles in ink were the numerals 4-4-2 and 4-5-6. His hands were red and sore, but he was proud of his journey and making his mark. Zander had become familiar with that pain. He was also familiar with the pain that comes from falling out of trees, when bucked from the broncos in the corral. In the gym, he was used to the post-workout muscle fatigue and aches. While in the ring, he was used to the side hits, the uppercuts, the jabs, the punches, all followed by bloody lips, bloody noses, popped blood vessels in the eyes. The swelling, the ice packs, the redness, and the ever-changing colors of bruises. The headaches, the body aches—all of the aches. He knew pain and, in some instances, he welcomed it. His misplaced footing, unguarded jaw, his recklessness, all welcomed pain. They reminded him he needed to focus.

He held his side, putting pressure on the cut, and leaned back. Two spindle posts of the half-stair railing leading upstairs cradled his head. He closed his eyes. When he lifted his head to see her, she had turned from the table and was facing him. The left side of her face was in the shadows, the right visible in the remaining light coming in through the screen door. She said something, he thought it sounded like, "Let me see." She was coming toward him, reaching her hand out. He stood straight, the knife at his side. He watched her hand move slowly to him. He moved his hand away from his side as she unbuttoned the remaining buttons of his shirt. He wasn't ready for her hand to pull away his shirt from the cut where it had congealed in the blood; the pull of the material caused a fresh wave of pain. Instinctively, his arms went up to defend, his head went back, and he let out a sound he wasn't expecting. Neither was she. When he refocused, it felt like his eyes were vibrating in their sockets. He had put his hand around the back of her neck and felt the softness of her hair. His other hand held the knife and had coiled around her arm. He could feel she had some strength in her and admired it. He looked at her, but she didn't make eye contact with him. She seemed deeply focused, looking at his body, looking at his wound, the one she had inflicted. He knew she hadn't meant to hurt him, that she most likely thought he was Kit coming after her. He couldn't be angry with her. She had good instincts, another thing he admired. He tilted his head toward her, studying her face. He was so close to her. He followed the subtle arch of her eyebrows to the bridge of her nose, to her eyes. He looked at her cheekbones. The right one was swollen, and he could see a bruise beginning to form. He felt the anger in him rise again as he thought of Kit inflicting that on her. She spoke, but he didn't catch what she said. He looked to the kitchen. He couldn't hear Kit stirring. Zander's stomach sank as he realized that he had killed Kit.

She repeated what she had said. "We should go to the kitchen."

He relaxed his hand on her neck and flicked the knife toward the kitchen. "Go," he replied.

She walked ahead of him slowly, which gave him time to think. How was he going to protect her from seeing what he had done to Kit? When they got to the entrance of the kitchen, he moved quickly to her side to block her from turning on the light. She hesitated at his quick movement, but then she continued walking toward the other side of the kitchen. He wasn't sure how, but he was going to try to shield her as long as he could from her seeing Kit's body. When she made it to the other side, stumbling on the items on the floor, he flicked on the light with his elbow. For a moment he just stood there, watching her, here in her home. If only this had been a different night. If only he had Brad's ease and had talked with her more when he'd first met her, maybe he would've been in this kitchen with her under other circumstances. If only there wasn't a dead body on the floor. Zander looked at Kit's lifeless body. He had done a number on him. He needed to think and act fast. She was moving with ease now, sure of her actions. She opened a cupboard and took out a black bag, and she headed to the sink, but stopped and opened another cupboard where Zander could see glass bottles of various liquors and wines lined up. She reached up and grabbed a full one. He recognized the shape. Now she stood by the sink, letting the water run. He moved to her side of the kitchen island. He watched her remove her sweater and saw the pained look on her face. He realized that Kit must have hurt her badly. She put some sterilizer in a bowl of water and took a needle and thread out of the black bag. He had moved behind her and was looking at her, her camisole, and how her hair hung low on her face. Her reflection in the window showed she was staring out at the backyard. His arm brushing against hers as he reached for the bottle of alcohol, the bowl of sterilizer, and the needle and thread pulled her out of her reverie, and she turned to look at him. He placed the items on the counter. He was still holding the knife. He could only imagine what she was thinking. She wasn't saying anything, and he didn't know where to start.

Finally, she spoke. "You need to take that shirt off."

Zander stood up against the kitchen island and put the knife down on the countertop. He pulled one sleeve off with his hand behind his back. He felt the tear in his skin leak more blood. His jaw clenched as he balled up his shirt and put it on top of her black sweater. He saw her eyes glance for a moment at the knife, then they went back to him. He was very aware of their proximity to one another. He could feel her breath across his skin. She placed her hands on his side, one above the cut and the other below. She was sizing it up. He looked to his right where the bottle was. He put his boot on a rung of one of the stools under the island and pulled it out for her. She took the seat and sat back for a moment, and he took the opportunity to twist off the cap of the bottle and raise it up to his lips. He knew what was coming as she watched his chest, the inhale and exhale, and then the swig of whiskey. She had a cloth in her hand and was dabbing the blood around the cut with it.

She sized him up one more time, then said, "Okay," to no one.

She took the needle and thread in her hands. He raised the bottle back to his lips and swallowed, then put the bottle firmly back on the countertop. That was her signal. Her hands were cool, and he breathed hard as she pushed his flesh together and made the first needle hole, the thread sliding through. He watched her; he couldn't turn away. He focused on her look of concentration, her eyes, her mouth, her steady hands. He memorized the random freckles on her forehead and nose and along her upper cheekbones. He heard nothing from the other side of the kitchen. He was beginning to realize the mess he was in. As she continued to stitch him up, he began to plan what needed to be done. He felt a slowing down of her stitching and he looked down at the very neat line of tight black thread on his side, the one spot on his torso that didn't have a tattoo yet assigned to it. She was almost done, tying off the thread and reaching for the scissors. He watched her move. She glanced up at him briefly while holding the scissors, then snip. It was done. She pushed off the stool and went over to the sink to wash her hands. He picked up the cloth she'd used to mop his blood off his skin.

He moved, putting the cloth on top of the pile with her sweater and his work shirt and stood behind her. He moved his hands to hers. She didn't flinch or move from him. He lathered up his hands with hers, using the soap. She turned to him, and he moved his hand along her neck and jaw to get his blood off of her. He dampened her hair to remove that blood as well. She turned back to the sink and emptied the bowl with sterilizer in it. She turned the water off and moved away from him. She focused on packing up her bag and put it back in the cupboard. She headed to the back stairs off the kitchen.

As he turned, heading for the stairs, his eyes caught something on the floor. It was one of the three missing buttons from his shirt. He bent down and retrieved it and then looked around and saw another one just under a barstool beside the kitchen island. He picked that one up, and then spotted the last one by the door leading out to the mudroom. It had rolled to the door stop and had settled there. Zander had all three buttons in his hand, which he shook like dice as he climbed the stairs following Waverly.

Upstairs, standing in the hallway, he saw there were four doors, two on the right and two on the left. She was in the room closest to his right; he could hear her opening a door and then she was with him again in the hallway. He wanted to say something to her, he opened his mouth, but what was there for him to say? She held out a flannel jacket to him, he took it and gently eased it on; it was warm and soft. He buttoned up the jacket. It was a bit snug, and he rolled up the cuffs. He turned to say thank you, but she had already gone into a room on the left. He went in and recognized it as a bedroom, her bedroom. The room was eggshell in color with white trim, with decorative crown molding. The dark hardwood floors were the same as in the hall. She was in the walk-in closet. He watched her slowly pull a sweater over her head. Her body, like his, was getting cold. The adrenaline had seen her through. He looked around. The bed looked soft. He could see another door leading to a bathroom, and his eyes caught the edge of a claw-foot bathtub. In her bedroom, there was a chair with an ottoman by the large window. The chair was positioned to look out to the horse barn and the woods beyond. There was a blanket thrown over the arm of the chair, and he imagined her sitting there, looking out the window, wrapped in that blanket. He went over to it and touched it; it was soft. The pictures hanging on the walls were paintings of forest scenes, and one with a meandering stream caught Zander's eyes. A nightstand next to her bed held a lamp, an alarm clock, and a book, opened facedown to mark her page. He stood next to her nightstand and looked at the book. He let the buttons fall from the palm of his hand and onto the top of the nightstand, coming to rest at the base of the lamp. Then he turned and walked out of the room.

He went down the stairs to the kitchen, taking a quick look around. Still no movement from Kit's side of the island. Zander grabbed the pile of the cloth, her sweater, and his bloody work shirt and rolled the knife up into it. He looked at the whiskey bottle and grabbed that, then he headed to the phone that hung on the kitchen wall. He dialed 911 and then left the receiver of the phone dangling by the cord. He could hear the operator's voice. He glanced at Kit who lay prone on his back, dead. Zander made his way down the hall to the front door. The rain was still falling. Waverly was coming down the stairs, meeting him at the door. He couldn't think of anything to say. No, that was not true, his mind was screaming things he wanted to say, but he said nothing. He moved his hand to her face; her skin was soft. He looked at her lips, then into her eyes. He was not sure of himself, he was not sure what the end result would be with his actions, but he wasn't sure if he'd ever get this chance again. He moved his head in closer to her and kissed her. His fingers flexed on the back of her neck, applying pressure. His mouth felt hers and their reciprocated pressure. Then he let go and went through the screen door. He stooped to pick up the box of medicine and tucked it under his arm. He heard the screen door fall shut behind him. He didn't look back as he crossed the yard, heading for the road where the van was. He got into the van and took a breath. He needed to set things in motion. He looked at the clipboard. He'd forgotten to mark the start of the mileage. That was dumb luck. He looked at her package. He went into the rear of the van and placed it back on the shelf. He then took one of the plastic bags used for any broken or damaged items while in transit and put the clothes with the knife, cloth, and whiskey bottle in it and put the bag on the passenger seat. He ran his hand over his hair, brushing off the rain. He sat in the driver's seat and started the engine. He did a three-point turn and headed back the way he came, remembering the detour. The work crew who had set up the road-closed signs had moved off to another flooded area. At the covered bridge, he stopped the van. His head was swirling with what had just happened. He let the van idle and got out, letting the light rain fall on him. He went over to the guardrail and looked at the raging water. In his hand, he held his work shirt with the knife wrapped in it.

When Zander arrived at Farm & Pharma, he backed the van up in the secure area behind the building. He wiped down the front area with the sleeves of the flannel jacket and replaced the keys back in the secure lock box and not in the return lock box. The rain had let up some. He tucked the plastic bag that held the bloody cloth, her sweater, and the whiskey bottle under his arm and headed off in the direction of his apartment. Along the way on the darkened streets, he thought of his options. He could go to the police. Then he thought back to the time when he was seated outside the office of Easton's chief of police.

In the town of Easton, Kit had thrown a hammer through the window of Connor's Market. Earlier that day Kit had used much profanity to describe the items the shop was selling, and the owner had told Kit to leave the premises.

"Don't you know who the fuck I am, old man? You know who my father is, what do you think will happen to your crummy little store if you throw me out?" Kit yelled.

Some of the patrons exited the shop, clearly not wanting to be a part of this conversation, which they guessed would turn into an altercation.

The owner of the store, Lenny Connor, didn't back down, "I know who you are and who your father is, but this is my store. Now get, out!" He pointed with his index finger toward the door.

"You will pay for this!" Kit slid his arm along a shelf, and the merchandise it held crashed to the floor. Then he kicked open the door with his boot, breaking the metal casing of the doorplate.

It was the fall of their senior year at Gyrfalcon Academy, and Kit was in full force. The days of him doing nothing were coming to an end. His father, Harold Scott Mayfield, had paid a visit to the Academy on Fair-Weather Day. On Fair-Weather day, the parents or guardians of the new senior class came to the Academy to discuss the next steps of their soon-to-be graduate. Harold Scott Mayfield had just found out that Kit hadn't completed any of the college applications the guidance counselor at the Academy had garnered for Kit, and he had no intention of ever completing them.

Zander, who had been thinking of his future since coming to the Academy, had gotten a job in Easton on the Green. Weekends he was there helping out Lenny Connor the owner of Connor's Market, which was a little mom-and-pop shop with baked goods, canned goods, a deli, and a dairy section. Zander was saving his money in preparation for graduation. The night before Fair-Weather Day, Zander had been invited to the Thayer's for supper.

"Thank you for having me over for supper," Zander said to Natalie and Rupert Thayer as he sat down at the set dining room table. The gloss on the dark-stained table reflected the silver of the serving trays and bowls

Natalie had brought out for this occasion. The meal before them looked more like a feast to Zander. The salad, the warm homemade bread, the roasted chicken with red potatoes . . . Zander's mouth watered.

"It's been too long since you have been here for supper. I can't get over how much you have grown. You could barely fit on that sofa when you first arrived here, and you most certainly won't fit on it now," Natalie said as she served Zander his meal and sized him up. He had now reached the height and age where she figured there was a hollow leg on the boy, and she put a very generous helping on his plate of not only chicken but also salad, potatoes, and two rolls with a large glass of milk.

Rupert began the delicate conversation. "Zander, I know you've been working in Easton part time at the market. Tomorrow is Fair-Weather Day for the seniors—"

Zander cut in, "Oh don't worry I won't be hanging around the Academy. I signed up to work the afternoon."

"I'm not worried about you hanging around the Academy, Zander," Rupert said firmly, "You can be wherever you want to be. Don't even think you don't belong here just as much, if not more than the other boys."

"Sir, no Sir," Zander said feeling the harshness of Mr. Thayer's tone.

"I think what we're trying to say Zander is that if you'd like to be a part of the activities tomorrow, I'd be happy to represent your adult," Natalie said in a gentle tone.

Rupert added, "Yes, that is what I mean. We will both be happy to be there for you."

"Oh," Zander replied. "Well, I've already told Mr. Connor I'd work, and that's really where I should be."

"That's fine, dear," Natalie said.

"Speaking of work Zander, do you have any plans after graduation? Were you considering college, or perhaps travel?" Rupert asked.

"I thought I'd find a place in the city. More job opportunities there for me. Figure out what I want to do," Zander replied.

"Well, we can certainly help you with that Zander," Natalie stated. "We can help you look for an apartment, and we can definitely help you until you get on your feet."

"I appreciate the offer, Mrs. Thayer, but I've been saving up since I started working and I've got enough to get started," Zander replied.

Natalie looked to Rupert, who was putting dressing on his salad. He caught Natalie's look. "Oh, well yes, of course you have, that's very responsible of you Zander, but we are here for you should anything unexpected arise. And of course, you will have the remainder of the balance in your account."

Zander's keep while at the Gyrfalcon Academy had been minimal. He didn't ask for anything special, buying only the items that he needed for the school terms in way of pens, pencils, and notebooks. Unlike the other boys who, when given their allowances or extra spending money tucked into a card from a parent or grandparent, went off to purchase what Zander thought of as unnecessary clutter or sweets. Zander didn't ask Mr. Thayer for anything other than on Christmas and his birthday for enough to buy a few books. The topics of the books included westerns, nature, classics, and adventure books, and he read them—devoured them, really—and then re-read them. In his room, the textbooks from previous semesters were kept in the leather suitcase he had arrived with.

"So, what do you plan on doing for the day tomorrow besides working?" Rupert asked Zander. Natalie was placing another freshly baked roll on Zander's plate when he looked up at Rupert. He hadn't really thought of the hours before work and how to fill them. He gave a slight shrug and a deep, "Hmmm," which translated to, *I don't know.*

"Well, how about you take one of the Academy's bikes for the day. I know there's a two-hour limit, but with everything else going on here tomorrow, I don't think we will miss one bike for the day. What do you think?" Rupert suggested.

"Thank you, Sir, that's very nice of you," replied Zander.

"What a great idea! These old roads have such lovely woods and fields. The scenery is just beautiful," added Natalie.

On his walks into town and back to the Academy, Zander had taken in the nature that was in the area. Zander often went into the woods surrounding the Academy for walks and to have some time to himself with nature. With a bike for the whole day, he'd be able to explore other roads and see other sights. He had not been dreading tomorrow, but not looking forward to the day either. He didn't need any reminders that he was an orphan. Now, though, he was looking forward to doing a little exploring.

"Do be careful though, Zander," Natalie warned. "Not everyone drives the speed limit on these back roads."

Zander swallowed a piece of buttered roll and replied, "I will, Mrs. Thayer."

"Perfect!" exclaimed Mr. Thayer. "I'll let Jerry know in the morning that you're approved to have a bicycle for the day then."

Zander left the Thayer's house and walked across the quad toward his dorm. The evening was warm with a slight breeze, the daylight still lingering in the sky. Zander stopped for a moment, looking up at the early stars. He appreciated the Thayer's. Not once had they treated him as an orphan or cast a look of pity on him. He was very full, thinking of the table that had been set before him and his plate heaped with food. He wondered where Scrabble, Natalie's cat, was. Usually, she would've been all over him as soon as he came through the door, and how could she resist that chicken smell? He wondered where she had gone. He pushed through the dorm door and bounced up the stairs. He could hear some voices in the common room. Lights out would be soon. He walked to his room and readied himself for bed.

The sun was bright on Fair-Weather Day. Zander's bike was ready for him. Jerry, the Academy's handyman, had even rigged a headlight and new reflectors on it. Zander peddled down the long drive of the Academy, past cars with families arriving for the day. He took a swift left turn, heading in the direction of Easton. He saw the usual road before him and then he swayed to the left, taking a new road. He stopped before a covered bridge and leaned the bike on the guardrail. He looked down at the rippling stream below, watching the water splash off the rocks. He walked the bike over the covered bridge, looking between the planks at the water below him. It was cooler in the bridge; the smell of wood reminded him of the logging camp in Alaska just outside of the borough where he lived. He watched as the last of the season's swallows flew in and out of the entrance to the bridge. He exited just as a pickup truck came at him, moving fast. He quickly moved his bike out of the way. The driver blew his horn at Zander, and it echoed through the tunnel of the bridge. Zander barely made out a logo on the side of the truck—it started with an M. As the dust from the truck settled, he flung a leg over the bike and began pedaling. He coasted down little hills, stopping to admire the forests, stone walls, and animals he caught glimpses of. Approaching a neatly maintained stone wall, he heard music playing. He slowed his bike down when he saw a man and a woman swaying to the soft music coming from the open set of French doors that led onto the porch where the couple danced. Zander put a foot on the ground, stopping the bike and watched them sway. Eventually he pushed off again, not wanting to disturb this moment they were sharing, a moment that reminded Zander of his parents and how he'd catch them in the kitchen on the nights his father came home from working on the pipe. He'd be gone for days, but on the nights when he returned home, after supper his parents would dance in the kitchen.

He was making good time and had twenty minutes to kill before his shift started. He rode the bike around the Town Green a couple of times and waved to the older guys playing chess together as they did every time he was in town. He waved to a couple of women sitting on the other benches, watching their young children play in the grass near them. He watched a woman who he had seen before in town exit the post office with Cal, one of the local mail delivery guys, who carried a bunch of packages for her. *What could be in all those boxes?* He took a left leaving the Green and pulled his bike into the alley behind Lenny's shop. He went into the back of the store and called out to Mr. Connor, letting him know he was there.

"You're early, lad," Lenny yelled back through the doorway that separated the stockroom from the sales area.

"Where should I start?" Zander asked.

Lenny was a stout man with thick, bushy eyebrows. He always wore a short-sleeved, button-down shirt, even in the winter, and the hair on his forearms was as black as the thinning hair on his head. He wore thick bifocal glasses, but still had trouble reading fine print. Lenny pulled a clipboard from under the cashier's desk and set it on his round stomach. He flipped through the top two pages. "Well, I made a dent in the inventory and the restock items. Business was slow this morning. So, you can go ahead and start pulling the needed items from the shelves and boxes and bring them out here to restock."

Zander took the clipboard from Lenny, turning to go back into the shelves full of stock. Lenny called out to him, "Hey kid if anything's too heavy don't bother with it, be careful."

Zander didn't respond, but he smiled a little at the thought. Lenny had thrown his back out one too many times and couldn't lift like he used to. Zander had the confidence of youth on his side and hadn't met anything in the stockroom he couldn't take on.

Lost in his work, Zander quietly and swiftly moved from the stockroom to the selling floor, but he perked up when Lenny called to him, "Alright, get ready. In the next ten minutes we will have a slew of customers, and if I need anything I'll call out to you to get it from the shelves." Lenny was always right when it came to the timing for a rush of customers to hit the store.

Toward the end of the day, Zander was well into the back of the stockroom when he heard a commotion from the sales floor. He turned his head to the side. He recognized the voice that was yelling obscenities in the store. It was Kit Mayfield. By the time Zander got through the maze of boxes to the doorway Kit had already left, leaving the front door broken.

Lenny held up his hands in a calming motion to the remaining customers in the shop. "It's alright now. Just a hot head. Some apples don't fall far from the tree. It's okay, Mrs. Gillis, I can help you in one moment." Lenny went over to the broken door and pried off the broken bit that would need replacing, then turned to Zander. "I'm going to need you to run over to Whitmeyer's hardware and get a replacement piece for that door. Can you do that for me?" Lenny took out a folded-over wad of money with a metal money clip from his pants pocket and took off a fifty-dollar bill, handing it to Zander along with the broken metal piece. Zander headed out of the store, running down the street to the next block, then crossed the street and ran into the single-story stand-alone Whitmeyer's Hardware. Seth Whitmeyer was at the register reading the newspaper, and he looked up to see who had just burst through his store door in such a hurry. As if there could be a hardware emergency, but today was that day!

Zander spoke through short breaths, "Hi, Mr. Whitmeyer. Mr. Connor needs a new one of these for the store door." Zander held out the broken metal piece in his hand for Mr. Whitmeyer to see.

Mr. Whitmeyer folded the paper haphazardly, came around the counter, and took the door latch's strike plate from Zander's hand. "Alright boy, aisle five. Let's go."

Zander walked beside Mr. Whitmeyer, who walked with an uneven gait.

"Now if I remember correctly, his door has an under and over lock, and it's not the standard size."

As Mr. Whitmeyer adjusted his bifocals, looking at the wall with pegs sticking out of it, he asked, "What happened that would have caused the damage?"

"There was a disruption," Zander replied.

Mr. Whitmeyer turned his head to look at Zander who was almost eye to eye with the older man.

"A disruption you say. Wouldn't have anything to do with another young boy from your school now, would it?" Mr. Whitmeyer may have been holding the newspaper when Zander entered the hardware store, but Zander had noticed that the newspaper was upside down. A few moments earlier, Mr. Whitmeyer had been looking out the window by the check-out desk and watched as Kit Mayfield took the steps two at a time leading up to Lenny's store and flung the door open. Mr. Whitmeyer shook his head. Everyone in the town of Easton was familiar with that shuffling walk of Kit Mayfield—and his temper.

Mr. Whitmeyer tucked his thumbs into his suspenders and waited for the storm to pass. He could only imagine what was going on inside that store and he was happy Kit had not decided to come into the hardware store. Moments later Mr. Whitmeyer watched Lenny's door fling open with such force that he heard the crack of wood giving way, and saw Kit exiting the store yelling, his shouts echoing through the Town Green. Mr. Whitmeyer shook his head, looking down to the floor, only now realizing he was wearing two different shoes. When he looked up again, he saw a tall young man running toward the hardware store. Not one to let on that he kept a watchful eye on the happenings of Easton, he settled himself in the chair behind the counter and busied himself with the newspaper.

Mr. Whitmeyer didn't wait for Zander to answer his question as he pulled the correct door latch strike from one of the metal pegs. "Alright then, you might also need a fuller backing, just in case there was damage to the door frame." Mr. Whitmeyer moved a bit to the right and slid the item he was speaking of off a peg. "Let's head up to the counter to get you a small bag."

Zander trailed behind Mr. Whitmeyer up to the front of the store. Mr. Whitmeyer went behind the counter, putting the items on the top, and reached for a small brown bag. As he flapped the bag open, he stopped and turned to Zander.

"You know if Mr. Connor has a screwdriver and tools to fix this?"

Zander looked at Mr. Whitmeyer with a blank expression on his face and mumbled, "I don't know, sir."

Mr. Whitmeyer tucked the bag back into its slot and then pulled out a medium-sized one. "That's okay, he might, but just in case, he can borrow this screwdriver. I'll put in this hammer and here's some sandpaper in case there's rough edges left behind. When he's done with them, you can just bring them back here. If I'm closed up for the night because tonight is my card-playing night, just leave them in the mailbox out front. No one will bother them."

"Yes, sir," Zander replied. He went to put the fifty-dollar bill on the countertop next to the items.

"Put that away, boy. Tell Mr. Connor we've all been there. Now off you go and be careful crossing the street."

"Thank you, sir, I will." Zander put the money in his pants pocket and took off through the door, running as soon as his feet hit the sidewalk. He slowed to look both ways, but there was never much traffic in Easton, so he crossed the street with ease and ran back to the store.

Zander waited until Mr. Connor wasn't with a customer and then spoke with him. "Here, sir. Mr. Whitmeyer said no charge, that 'we've all been there.'" He held out the money to Lenny.

"He's a good man there. Unfortunately, he's right, we have all been right where I am, and I think there's more incidents to come."

Lenny didn't take the money. Instead, he asked, "Can you stay a bit late tonight? I'd like to have the door fixed after we close, and you know how my wife gets when I'm late for supper. Tonight, we are going to that new movie that just opened up at the theater, so I can't be late. You think you could fix that door?"

Zander looked to the door and saw the splinters of wood sticking out. Mr. Whitmeyer was right about what supplies were needed. "Yes, I can stay and fix it."

"Good boy. Keep the money. That will be for your work. Just lock up the shop and leave through the back door," replied Mr. Connor, slapping Zander on the back.

"Would it be okay if I use the phone? I should let Mr. Thayer know I'll be late getting back to the Academy."

"Of course and tell him that if he has any questions to just let me know," Lenny said.

Zander called the Academy. It was close to 5 p.m., but the secretary answered the phone. "Gyrfalcon Academy, how may I assist you?" Loretta "Lottie" Turner was a true secretary. She took her job seriously. She was a single working mother, which to her meant she had to juggle multiple things in her day, and she wanted to do that with grace and ease. She found ways to be prepared for anything and had excellent time management skills and the patience of a saint. She was a petite Southern belle with curves. Her strawberry blonde hair was always perfectly coiffed. She looked like she had stepped out of a Hitchcock film.

"Hello Ms. Turner, it's Zander Blake. I'm a student there."

"Oh honey, I know who you are. You okay, darlin'?" Lottie replied in her thick Southern accent.

"I'm fine. I have to stay late at Mr. Connor's shop to help out and close up. I just wanted to let Mr. Thayer know because I have one of the school bikes."

"Oh, I'm sure it won't be a problem. I think he's in the dining hall with the students and their parents—" her voice trailed off as she remembered Zander's situation. She turned her tone and the conversation. "I will grab him before he leaves for the night and give him the message. You just be careful. Perhaps I should see if he can come get you?"

"No, please don't. I don't want to bother him. I'll be fine. The bike has a light and reflectors. I shouldn't be that late anyway."

"Alright, then, sugar, I'll let him know. I'll see you Monday then."

"Yes, Ms. Turner." Zander hung up the phone.

When Lenny flipped the sign on the storefront door from open to closed, Zander came out of the stockroom and looked at the doorframe. He got the bag that Mr. Whitmeyer had packed up with the tools and pieces and began using the screwdriver to take the remaining screw, which had been bent, out of the doorframe.

"You gonna be okay here?" Lenny asked, looking at his watch.

"I'll be fine. It won't take me long." Zander had already removed the screw and was sanding down the splintered wood to make a smooth surface for the extra backing.

"Alright then. Just remember to lock up the door after it's fixed, then leave through the back and lock up that door."

"I will," Zander replied, still sanding away at the splintered wood. Lenny left through the back door. Shortly after, Zander heard a car start up and rattle out of the alleyway to the street.

When Zander finished with the door, he made sure it swung in place and that the deadbolt lined up with the new plate. It clicked in place. Satisfied with the work he had done, he gathered up the tools, putting them in the bag Mr. Whitmeyer had put them in and he then turned out the store's front light. Out the back door he went into the alley, and, twisting the doorknob's lock in place, he pulled the door tightly shut. He put the bag in the bicycle basket and walked it out of the alleyway to the sidewalk. Rounding the corner, he saw that Mr. Whitmeyer's storefront, along with the other ones around the Town Green, were dark. He peddled over to Mr. Whitmeyer's mailbox, put the bag in it, and then pushed off, pedaling toward the Academy. He'd be too late for dinner, but he remembered there was some milk and cereal in the common room. He clicked on the bike's headlight and breathed in the night air. Behind him, a thin figure who had been watching Zander stepped out of the shadows.

Zander chose the familiar road he usually walked to get back to the Academy. There were a few bends and turns, but he knew the road well. It was a straight shot to the Academy and also had a covered bridge. He had just turned the bike to go over the covered bridge when from behind him he heard sirens and saw the flashing lights of the chief of police's car bounce off of the side of the covered bridge. Zander got off of the bike and pulled it far over to the guardrail, giving the chief's car enough room to pass, but the car came to a stop right in front of him. Chief Mel Raymond stepped out of the car and looked at Zander.

"Where you going so late, boy?" asked the chief as he exited his car.

"Back to the Academy," Zander replied.

"Doubt you're supposed to be out this late, and doubt that's your bike," he said, linking his thumbs through his belt loops. Zander remained quiet. "Where'd you come from?"

"I was working late at Lenny Connor's shop, the Market," Zander answered.

"Is that so? Because I saw Lenny and his missus leave a while ago. I doubt Lenny would leave the likes of you in his shop alone."

"I work for him." Zander started making fists with his hands in his pockets. The chief's reputation of being hard handed had reached all of the boys at the Academy.

"Oh, I know all about you." Zander's reputation as an outsider to Easton preceded him. "Get in the back of the car," Chief Raymond ordered.

"What for?" asked Zander.

"You telling me no?" Chief Raymond was releasing the handcuffs from behind his back. As he approached Zander, he was able to get a better look at the one he called boy. As Zander pushed off the guardrail, showing his full height, he removed his hands from his pockets and took a stance.

"You're gonna want to think twice about what's rollin' around in that head of yours, son."

Chief Raymond should've been promoted to a cushy desk job with all the time he had on the force but had been kept in his swivel seat in Easton's Police Station and the Mayfield's pockets for the last ten years. He could handle the wiry boys at the Academy, the few troublemakers in town, but looking at Zander he wasn't ready for a rough and tumble with this guy and hoped his words would dissuade him. Chief Mel Raymond was a large man in all respects. His belt and holster could barely be seen under the girth of his stomach. He walked everywhere like he owned the town of Easton and was above the law. Those who had known the chief as an officer both felt and saw the change in him and knew the Mayfield's had a part in his actions. His sandy blonde hair was covered by his campaign hat. He had long ago stopped maintaining the police officer's clean-cut appearance and had a few days' worth of scruff on his face. His eyes were tan-yellow, and when he smirked his teeth showed years of coffee and nicotine stains. Zander really didn't have a choice, and there was no use in attempting to plead his case. Zander turned so Chief Raymond could put the cuffs on him, and he felt the hand of the Chief help spin him on his shoulder. "That's the way to go," breathed the Chief in Zander's ear. His breath smelled of stale coffee.

"What about the bike?" asked Zander.

"Evidence, coming with us," Chief Raymond responded.

Chief Raymond patted Zander down. The Chief removed the crumpled fifty-dollar bill that Lenny had paid Zander from his pocket.

"And just what is this? You thieving scum!"

Chief Raymond grabbed Zander harshly by the back of the head and shoulder and pushed him into the back of the car, slamming the door. The cuffs cut into his wrists. He watched as Chief Raymond was barely able to lift the bike into the trunk of the patrol car. Once the trunk slammed, the chief settled in the driver's seat and radioed the station. "I got him. Get started on the paperwork."

When they pulled up to the police station, Zander looked out at the darkened streets of Easton. Lenny Connor's store was lit up and a police car with its lights on was parked in front. A couple of officers were standing outside, and one was sweeping up debris from the sidewalk. When Zander was pulled out of the backseat of the car, he looked to Lenny's store, saw the broken front window, and realized that's what the officer was sweeping up.

Zander and the chief walked through the door of the police station; a few police officers were working at their desks. Zander was pushed down into a chair by the chief at Officer Jebidiah Hayden's desk.

"Have at him, Hayden. I'm gonna get some coffee," said the chief.

Zander looked at Officer Hayden. "How old are you?" Officer Hayden asked.

"Seventeen," Zander replied.

"I know you're an orphan, but who's your guardian?" asked Officer Hayden.

For a moment Zander pictured Emil's face. "No one," he mumbled.

"Gotta be someone who's responsible for you while you're here," insisted Officer Hayden.

Ms. Turner made her way to the auditorium, but it was empty. The click of her pumps echoed down the hall to the cafeteria, where she could hear the murmur of voices. She pushed through the large wooden doors and scanned the raised platform where the teachers ate. She could not see Mr. Thayer. She then scanned the room to see if he was mingling with the remaining parents, but she did not see his figure. Mrs. Fisher came up to her side. "Something wrong?"

"Oh no, just need to speak to Mr. Thayer," replied Ms. Turner.

"Oh, he left a little while ago. Only a handful of parents are left, and we can escort them out after dinner," responded Mrs. Fisher.

"Did you hear the disruption earlier?" asked Ms. Turner.

"No, what disruption?" asked Mrs. Fisher.

"Mr. Mayfield and his son, Kit, were discussing Kit's plans for after the Academy. Well, not so much discussing as Mr. Mayfield informing Kit what would be expected of him. It didn't go so well," Ms. Turner stated.

"I bet not. We've all heard Kit talking about taking a year or so break after graduation and traveling. I'm sure it was a rude awakening for Kit," stated Mrs. Fisher.

"Kit stormed out of the auditorium with Mr. Mayfield bellowing after him. Mr. Thayer had to deal with Mr. Mayfield and try to talk Kit down, but Kit left with his car," ended Ms. Turner.

"How did you hear about this?" asked Mrs. Fisher.

"How did you not hear it? They were so disruptive," stated Ms. Turner.

"I was in the auditorium for most of the day, and I missed it. I am always amazed at how you have your finger on the pulse of the academy," replied Mrs. Fisher, in true awe of Ms. Turner.

"Well, I'd better be going. I need to get this message to Mr. Thayer. Have a good rest of the night. See you Monday," called Ms. Turner over her shoulder as she headed down the hall.

"You have a great weekend. See you Monday, Lottie."

The women parted ways, Ms. Turner moving through the wooden doors and Mrs. Fisher working the room with the remaining parents.

Ms. Turner grabbed her light coat and purse, clicking off the hall lights but leaving the sconces on, and exited through the main doors. The night was cool, but the fresh air felt wonderful. The Fair-Weather festivities were always time consuming and stressful for most at the Academy, staff, students, and parents alike. But Lottie was prepared; she was diligent in her work and considered herself fortunate to have such a good job that afforded her a home and what her little girl needed. She walked to her car in the staff parking lot and turned the engine. She headed in the direction of the Thayer's house. Upon arriving, she left the car running, exited the car, clicked up the porch steps, and rang the doorbell. She smoothed her skirt just in time to greet Natalie.

"Natalie, so sorry to bother you, but I have a message for Rupert," said Lottie.

"Oh, come in Lottie," Natalie held the door open for her to come in.

"I can't, thank you though, my girl is waiting for me at home," responded Lottie.

"Well, Rupert left to go to his card game at the Germaine's. Is it something urgent?" asked Natalie.

"Oh no, it's from student Zander Blake, he phoned saying he was going to help close Lenny's store and will be later than expected that's all," replied Lottie.

"Very responsible of him to call," Natalie observed.

"He's a different one, that one. Always so polite and thoughtful," commented Lottie.

"I'll let Jerry know up in the garage to expect the bike later. Thank you for letting me know. I'll tell Rupert when he gets home," said Natalie.

"Anytime Natalie," said Lottie.

"Soon we will have to get together to catch up," Natalie commented as she stepped out onto the porch with Lottie.

"Yes, before the holidays. Have a lovely weekend, Natalie," said Lottie as she got into her car.

"You as well Lottie. Good night," Natalie called after her.

Lottie headed to her home in Weston. When approaching the covered bridge, Lottie saw the lights of the chief's car and slowed. Her body stiffened at the thought of Chief Raymond. She hoped all of her lights were working, that there'd be no excuse to pull her over and lean in her window. Her car was old, but reliable. Unfortunately, with the age, wear and tear began to wreak havoc on her purse. Chief Raymond with his ticket book had suggestions of how she could make the ticket disappear. Lottie out of the corner of her eye looked briefly toward where the Chief was standing outside his patrol car. She didn't linger and made the turn to Weston.

Natalie looked at the neatly written message from Lottie to Rupert. She watched as the taillights went down the drive. She noticed the one on the passenger side was out again. Natalie made a mental note to tell Lottie on Monday about it. Her mind went back to Zander being late and thought automatically about supper for him, knowing he had missed dinner at the assembly. She went to the kitchen and began making him a sandwich. While spreading mayo on the bread, she dialed the Germaine's number on the kitchen phone and continued to move around the kitchen making Zander's meal.

"Hello, Germaine residence," Ingrid Germaine, Natalie's best friend, answered.

"Hi, Ingrid, it's Nat. How's the game going?" Natalie asked.

"Oh, you know, who knows? There's more chatting than cards being played. How did the day go?" responded Ingrid.

"Good, only one small hiccup. I'm sure Rupert has filled you in," replied Natalie.

"I've been cleaning and getting the house ready for Waverly. She comes home this weekend. So, I haven't really been listening. I can't wait to see her. She's grown up so much," replied Ingrid. "I can't believe she's a sophomore in high school.

"She really has. I can't believe she'll be abroad in the spring," replied Natalie in amazement.

"These kids have so many more options, its good she's taking advantage of them. So, what happened?" asked Ingrid.

"Well, it was Harold and Kit Mayfield. Kit wants to travel and take time off after graduating. But you know as well as I do that Harold has plans for his boy and he'd hear nothing of it from Kit," Natalie began.

"I think everyone, but Kit knows Harold has plans for him," Ingrid chimed in.

"It's sad that their relationship is so strained," Natalie stated.

"So, supper here Saturday? I know Waverly would love to see both you and Rupert," Ingrid asked.

"Perfect, I'll bring dessert," Natalie agreed.

"You want to speak to Rupert?" Ingrid asked.

"Just for a moment," Natalie confirmed.

"Okay, hold on." Ingrid put the phone receiver on top of the phone and walked out of the kitchen down the hallway and to the living room where a card table and chairs had been set up. The sideboard had glasses, a bucket of ice, some snacks, and full liquor decanters. As she poked her head into the room, she brushed a few errant strands of pale blonde hair out of her dark blue eyes. Her high cheekbones showed a flush from the activity of cleaning the upstairs and readying it for her daughter's arrival. Her cupid's bow lips gave a smile as a roar of laughter came from the table. There occupying the chairs were Arthur Germaine, Rupert Thayer, Seth Whitmeyer Nick O'Dell, and Tommy Haskins.

"Rupert, Nat's on the phone," Ingrid said with a smile at the men seated at the table as the laughter subsided. She then turned and headed back upstairs to continue making her daughters bed, smiling as she went.

Rupert left the table, chuckling a little to himself as he picked up the phone.

"Hey love," he said into the receiver.

"Sorry to break up your winning streak," Natalie teased. "Zander left a message with Lottie earlier that he was going to be later than expected because he's going to close up the shop for Lenny. I'll call Jerry and let him know not to wait for Zander," Natalie explained to Rupert. "Think he'll be okay riding the bike back?" she asked.

"He should be fine. Jerry put lights on the bike and new reflectors this morning," responded Rupert.

"I'm making him a sandwich. I'm going to bring it up to the dorm for him. The rest of the parents are leaving now," Natalie said.

"Sounds good, love," Rupert said. "I'll see you in a while."

"Have fun, dear," Natalie said.

Zander returned Officer Hayden's stare. "Headmaster Thayer," he stated.

Officer Hayden called the Academy. It was late, but there was a chance the headmaster might still be in his office. The nightshift security guard, Simon, who when not stationed at his desk in the Admissions building strolled the grounds, checking the dorms and buildings, answered the phone. "Hullo Gyrfalcon Academy."

"Hi Simon, Officer Hayden here. Rupert Thayer still there?" asked Officer Hayden.

"No, he left a while ago. Headed to the Germaine's," Simon said.

"Oh, okay. Thanks, Simon," Officer Hayden said as he hung up the phone.

Simon put the receiver down. He was just about to start another round. He walked down the corridor of the Admissions building, twirling his flashlight, and whistling, not giving the phone call from the police station a second thought.

In the police station, Officer Hayden looked at Zander and sighed. Friday nights were the Germaine's card game night, a regular for years. Mr. Mayfield's regular card game night was Thursday, one Officer Hayden had recently been accepted into the fold of. Officer Hayden was tipped back in his chair. Now he came forward and flipped through the phone book to the Germaine's number, picked up the phone, and spun the dial. As he dialed, he wondered why the two card games weren't ever combined. *Why didn't the players of one mingle with the other?* It would never happen.

No sooner had Rupert hung up the phone than it began to ring again.

"Hello, Germaine residence," Rupert said.

"May I speak with Mr. Rupert Thayer?" the voice said.

"This is," replied Rupert.

"This is Officer Hayden."

"What can I help you with, Officer Hayden?" asked Rupert.

"Well, sir, I have here at the station a student of yours. Seems like they are going to be charged with vandalism and theft," stated Officer Hayden.

Zander listened to the words Officer Hayden was saying and hoped Mr. Thayer would at least hear Zander out. Rupert guessed it was Kit and wasn't sure why he was being called, as he was positive Mr. Mayfield should be notified, but maybe they couldn't find him. "Have the boy's parents been notified?" asked Rupert.

"Well, that's the thing sir, the boy gave us your name," Hayden responded.

Rupert, now confused, hesitantly asked, with a knot in his stomach, "Who is the boy?"

"Zander Blake," stated Hayden.

"Let me talk to him," Rupert said flatly.

Officer Hayden held the phone up to Zander's ear. "Sir" he grumbled.

"Zander don't say a thing. I'm on my way," Rupert said and then hung up the phone.

"Hmm," Zander mumbled, confirming, and moved his head away from the phone. Officer Hayden went to talk to Rupert, but there was nothing but a dial tone.

"Well, okay then. Is he coming?" asked Officer Hayden as he replaced the receiver in the cradle.

Zander sat back in his chair and nodded his head yes.

Rupert hung up the phone and headed into the living room. "Sorry, fellas, I have to go. Apparently, the police in this town have nothing better to do."

"Everything alright?" asked Arthur.

"They've detained one of my students. Talking about charging him with some nonsense. Can we pick up next week?" Rupert asked as he headed for the door.

"Of course."

"Sure."

"This hand was crap anyway," came the responses from those seated around the table.

Mr. Whitmeyer rose and began collecting the glasses and plates the men had used and started shuffling to the kitchen. Nick and Tommy followed carrying items. Rupert was already in the mudroom off the kitchen pulling on his coat. Arthur asked, "You need any help?"

"Oh, no, it'll be sorted out. Thanks though," replied Rupert.

The men gave a quick handshake and Rupert went out into the night to his car. On the drive to the police station, Rupert hit the steering wheel. He'd forgotten to call Natalie and tell her he'd be late.

Ingrid came downstairs to see Mr. Whitmeyer leaving by the back door and her husband calling after him to be safe driving home.

"What happened? Someone run out of money?" she teased.

"No, Rupert got a phone call from the police station. One of the students has been picked up," Arthur responded. He walked over to the kitchen sink and began filling it with water to start washing the dishes.

"I bet it's Kit," she said.

"Maybe, but wouldn't Harold be called, not Rupert?" he asked.

"Good point. Did he call Nat and let her know?" asked Ingrid.

"He said he'd sort it out. Maybe it won't take long," Arthur said, not convincingly.

"Are you kidding? Chief Raymond will be using this to sound off everything wrong about the educational system, the teachers, how he and his force have better things to do than deal with those boys up on the hill."

"You're right. Rupert's going to be there all night," Arthur said with a sigh.

"I'm calling Natalie," Ingrid said.

Natalie had chilled the plate for the sandwich and wrapped it well in aluminum foil. She took a baggie and put some carrots and celery sticks in it, then looked at the bottles of apple juice on the shelf in the fridge and took one. She picked up the phone and dialed the number to the maintenance building. Jerry picked up.

"Maintenance, Jerry here."

"Hi Jerry, it's Natalie Thayer."

"Oh hello Mrs. Thayer. How's that porch swing working for you?"

"It's wonderful, Jerry. Thank you for making the time to paint it and re-hang it."

"My pleasure." Jerry was balancing the phone with his head and shoulder while his hands were busy greasing up a pipe fitting.

"Jerry, you know the bike that Zander took earlier today with Rupert's permission?"

"Ah-yup," he responded.

"Well, Zander had to stay late in town and will be bringing it back later than expected. I just wanted to let you know that he called and let us know, so it's alright. And I don't want you to feel like you have to stay late."

"Oh, well, sure. If it's okay with you and Mr. Thayer, then it's fine by me. If he brings it up here when he gets back, he can just lean it up against the building. No rain tonight so it should be fine up here until I come in tomorrow morning."

"Oh, thank you, Jerry. You have yourself a good night."

"You too, Mrs. Thayer." Jerry put the pipe fitting down on his workbench and hung up the phone. He wiped his hands, covered in grease, on the front of his coveralls. He looked around and nodded his head, then turned off the lights and called it a night.

Natalie pulled the door to the house closed and began walking across the quad to the student dorms. She saw Simon's flashlight. He saw her shadow and shone the flashlight in her eyes.

"Oh, sorry, Mrs. Thayer. You alright?"

"Oh, I'm fine, Simon. Just bringing a late supper to one of the boys who missed it. How have you been?" asked Natalie.

"Good. Good. We've had some nice weather. Makes it easier to walk the grounds," Simon responded.

"Yes, it is a lovely time of year," Natalie observed as she breathed in the fresh air.

"I'll walk with you if you don't mind. I should check in on the dorms. You sure do look out for these lads, Mrs. Thayer. You and Mr. Thayer both," Simon stated as he fell in step with Natalie.

"Well, they are under our care while here, all of us are substitutes for so many roles in their lives. We really do have a good bunch of staff here."

"It's a nice place to work."

"It is."

They reached the dormitory door and went through. It was noticeably quiet in the halls. The day's events had apparently worn out the students. Natalie went up the stairs and down the hall to Zander's room and Simon headed down the corridor to do rounds. Natalie opened the door, placed the sandwich on Zander's desk, and turned on the lamp. He shouldn't have to come back to a dark room. Closing the door behind her, she felt a bit lightheaded and took a moment to steady herself. It must've been from all the excitement of the day. She needed to get some supper. She walked slowly back out to the quad and headed for the porch lights she had turned on. As she got closer to her porch, she could see seasonal white moths floating around the lights. She went up the steps and through the door, being careful to not let in any of the pretty winged creatures. She should have been hungry considering she hadn't eaten since breakfast, but she found herself tired instead. The phone rang on the hall table. She pushed herself off the closed door and picked up the receiver.

"Hello, Headmaster Thayer's residence," she said.

"Hi, Nat. Just wanted to let you know Rupert had to go into Easton. He got a call from the police station. Apparently one of the students has been picked up for something," Ingrid Germaine said.

"Oh no. Was it Kit?" Nat asked.

"He didn't say, but we didn't want you to worry. He rushed out of here, and I figured I'd just give you a call," Ingrid said.

"Well, I appreciate it. I'll keep the lights on for him," Natalie responded.

"Alright, get some sleep and see you Saturday," Ingrid said.

"Night." Nat hung up the phone and looked around the hall and listened to the quiet house. *It'll be nice to have Waverly back, even if it's just for a little bit.* Her laughter would echo through the house when she visited. Natalie made her way up the stairs and readied for bed. She'd read a bit of her book while waiting for Rupert to come home.

When Rupert pulled into a parking spot on the side of the Town Green, he wondered when exactly there had been a change in how the town was run. He got out of his car, walked across the street to the police station, and went up the stairs, going through the heavy door to another flight of stairs that he climbed, taking the left into the police station. Sitting with his back to the door was Zander, his hands cuffed behind his back.

Rupert couldn't hide his anger. "Officer Hayden, remove those cuffs. He's a kid!" Rupert exclaimed.

"Actually, no he's not. He may be a student, but he's old enough to be charged with what we have against him." Chief Raymond came out of his glass-walled office, holding a mug filled with coffee.

"What exactly are the charges?" asked Rupert.

"We have it on good authority that this cretin threw a hammer through Lenny Connor's store window. Vandalism," Chief Raymond held up a plastic evidence baggie with a fifty-dollar bill in it. "We also have him on theft. This money was taken from the cash register. We're trying to track down Lenny to make sure nothing else was stolen." Chief Raymond was smug with his response. "Oh, and theft of this." Chief Raymond snapped his fingers at the police officer sitting nearby who hopped up and retrieved the bicycle from around the corner.

"Chief," Rupert started, "Zander had my full permission to have that bike for the day."

"Well of course you would say that. I'm sure you don't want a scandal at the Academy. The Academy where you are the headmaster," replied the chief.

"Jerry will confirm it as well. Secondly, there's no way Zander vandalized Lenny's store. No way. He's been working there all year and has a good rapport with Lenny and the customers," Rupert stated.

"I heard the boy caused a ruckus today in the store. Couldn't get his way about something. Probably didn't want to work as hard as Lenny needed him too," the chief said.

"You couldn't be more wrong. I'm sure of it," Rupert said flatly.

Zander, meanwhile, sat quietly. Even with Mr. Thayer trying to sort things out, he knew he was going to take the fall for this. He hoped Mr. Connor would be home soon from the movies. Maybe that would make a difference.

"I'd like to talk privately with Zander," Rupert said, pulling Zander up by his arm. "And remove these ridiculous handcuffs!"

Chief Raymond came toward Zander, plunking his mug on Officer Hayden's desk. He reached for his keys and spun Zander around. Zander was now face to face with Mr. Thayer. He looked him in the eyes. Zander's reflected shame and embarrassment for putting Mr. Thayer in this position. Mr. Thayer's reflected kindness and tried to reflect reassurance. Zander felt the cuffs give way from his wrists. He brought his hands forward and rubbed his wrists, which were red from the cuffs.

"Those can go on just as quickly as they came off. You best remember that, boy," Chief Raymond said, snapping the cuffs closed.

Officer Hayden held out his arm to lead Mr. Thayer and Zander to a private room. Once inside and with the door closed Zander went to apologize, but Rupert cut him off.

"Don't worry about the bike, that will be taken care of. Everyone knew you were to have it today with permission. The store window, the fifty-dollar bill, and the incident in the store today. What are those about?" Rupert asked.

"The incident in the store happened in the early afternoon. I was in the stockroom when I heard the commotion between Mr. Connor and . . . ," Zander's voice trailed off.

"And?" Rupert pressed.

"Kit," Zander said.

"Kit," Rupert repeated.

"I came out of the stockroom to the sales floor and saw Kit kick the front door, damaging it," recounted Zander.

Rupert was rubbing a hand on his forehead. "Well, what happened to the window?"

"I don't know, sir. I fixed the door, made sure the store was locked up, which is where the fifty dollars came from. Mr. Connor gave it to me for staying late and for fixing the door. I returned the tools to Mr. Whitmeyer's mailbox and then I started to ride home," Zander responded.

"Did anyone see you leave?" asked Rupert.

"No, sir," Zander replied.

Natalie saw headlights go across her bedroom ceiling. She got out of bed and looked out the window. It was getting late, and Rupert still wasn't home. The car headed straight for the student's parking lot, where in any given year only a handful of seniors were allowed to have cars and only a handful could afford them. She sighed. She guessed that would be Kit coming back after blowing off some steam following the argument with his father. *Well at least he made it back safely and wasn't wrapped around a tree.* She sat on the edge of the bed, wondering what was taking so long at the police station. She watched the dark figure out the window, lit by the academy's lights, walk toward the dorms. Maybe Rupert would be home soon, as Kit was probably the cause for Rupert to be at the police station in the first place.

Zander remembered the events of that day and night with such clarity. He was put on probation his senior year by Chief Raymond with the condition of no further incidents and he would be able to graduate. It was a lesson for Zander, sent loud and clear from the police and Mr. Mayfield. It didn't matter that Mr. Thayer, Jerry, Lenny, and Mr. Whitmeyer all stood up for Zander. Mr. Mayfield stood against him. His senior year he was constantly looking over his shoulder knowing his every move was being watched. When graduation day came, Zander wasn't proud or excited like his classmates, he was relieved that his probation was over.

Zander twisted the key into the entry door of his apartment building and went through the partition doors. He remembered his laundry. He dashed down the hallway to the basement stairs. He grabbed his wet laundry and the bag, shoving everything into it. He slung the bag over his shoulder and went up the stairs. He listened on the lower step of the first flight, looking up through the railings of the stairs to see if anyone was there, but he didn't hear anyone. He ran up the flights to his apartment. Once inside, he put down everything he was carrying and breathed a sigh.

"Focus," he said aloud. He didn't waste time, he couldn't. He had to move quickly. He pulled a large black duffel bag out from under his bed. He turned and went into the kitchen and got a garbage bag, throwing the wet clothes into it. He emptied the three-drawer plain dresser that came with the apartment, dividing the clothing into piles to take and toss. He didn't have much in the way of food. Whatever there was, he tossed into a trash bag. Any snacks for travel he put in his backpack, which he grabbed off the floor and put on the kitchen counter. He took all of his personal items out of the kitchen drawer where he kept them and put them in the backpack. He systematically opened every drawer and emptied whatever was in there, again separating into keep or toss piles. He poured what was left in the whiskey bottle down the drain and put the empty bottle, along with the bloody cloth she had used on him, in a garbage bag. Her black sweater lay on the kitchen counter. He held it, running his hands over the softness of it, then he put it in his backpack.

When done in the kitchen, he looked under the bed and moved furniture, not that there was much, and then went into the bathroom. He turned on the shower and let the water run for a bit to get warm. He pulled off his clothes. There was blood on his pants from Kit. He threw all of the clothes he had been wearing into a garbage bag. When he entered the shower, he washed carefully around the stitches and scrubbed the blood from his skin. His mind was surprisingly calm. Once out of the shower, he dried off and opened his medicine cabinet. Fortunately, he had enough gauze and bandages. He worked quickly and clenched his teeth when he pushed the gauze around the stitches. He put on a button-down shirt, boxers, and pants. He pulled on socks. Bending over was rough, and tying the laces on his boots took a few tries. When dressed he cleaned out the bathroom, leaving nothing behind. The rain had stopped. He gathered all the items to be ditched and headed back into the hall. He waited and listened, no one. He knew he was running out of time. Soon people would start milling in and out of their apartments. He quickly went down the stairs and out onto the sidewalk. There were only a few people on the other side of the street. They didn't take notice of him, just a guy carrying out the garbage. He went through the gate to the alley, heading to the back street where dumpsters lined both sides. Zander walked away from his apartment's dumpster to one located two buildings up and threw in his bags. Then he walked calmly back to the alley and through both sets of doors. Back in his apartment, he did one more sweep through. He was leaving nothing behind. He stood on top of the bare mattress and lifted a ceiling tile. From the concealed spot he removed some legal papers that he unfolded and looked at to make sure they were all there. Then he retrieved his passport and four stacks of $100 dollar bills. He replaced the tile. He pulled off a few hundreds and left them under the apartment keys on the nightstand. He threw the rest of money and the documents into his backpack. The apartment was barren to begin with, and now it was stark. He slipped on a pair of gloves to hide his hands, which were covered in cuts. Carefully, he swung his backpack over his shoulder, and carrying his duffel he went through the door. He could hear the sounds of people stirring behind their apartment doors as he made his way down the stairs. He had one more stop to make before he would be heading in a direction to a place, he never thought he'd see again.

It was the earliest hours of the morning, yet there was Bruce in his glassed-in guard area. He buzzed Zander in. The gym had a random handful of people in it. Zander nodded to Bruce and walked to where Mickey leaned on the ropes of one of the training arenas.

"You look like hell," Mickey said.

Zander sidled up next to him gave a glance at the two sparring in the ring, then looked to the locker rooms. "I need a word."

"Alright then. You two princesses keep dancing. I'll be back in a jiff," Mickey called to the two in the ring.

Zander and Mickey turned to the locker room and silently went through the doors. In the locker room, one guy was taking his time putting on his t-shirt. Mickey barked at him, "Get outta here." The man, his arm half in a sleeve, got out of the way. Now the locker room was empty. Mickey knew that when Zander asked for anything, he needed to wait until Zander was ready to start, so he leaned on the locker room doors and waited.

"I need to leave town. Here's pay for the next three months. It should tide you over until you can find a replacement fighter," Zander placed an envelope in Mickey's hands. Mickey, having been a bookie since he was seven and running money, knew there was more than three months of Zander's winnings in that envelope.

"And the extra? Zander, what's the extra for?" he asked.

Zander looked down at his boots. Mickey knew how to be discreet. People had asked about Zander, not just for his fighting but for personal information as well. Mickey hadn't given them an inch, not that he knew much. Zander had to give Mickey the warning that people—police— might be coming around. They were never wanted in a boxing gym. There was a different kind of law and order within these walls.

"There may be some uniforms asking about me," Zander mumbled.

"You don't need to pay for my silence, or anyone else's here, Zander," Mickey said, holding out the envelope to Zander.

"Then for the inconvenience," Zander stated, not reaching for the money.

"Eh, what's a few coppers around? Nothing we can't handle here. You need anything from us?" Mickey asked, sliding the envelope into the inside pocket of his jacket.

Zander sighed. Here he was, leaving the gym and Mickey without a fighter for the weekend, loss of money both on the tables and under, and Mickey was asking if he could help Zander.

"No, Mickey. Thank you for taking me under your wing. I've learned a lot from you," Zander said.

"It was my pleasure. You've got the focus and the strength to continue. You're welcome back here any time," stated Mickey.

The men shared a brief hug and pats on the back. Mickey knew not to ask Zander for a reason or ask a question he had no right to ask. Granted, there were fights lined up with Zander as the lead, but it wasn't anything Mickey couldn't finagle around. He just hoped that whatever Zander was leaving for or from, he would be alright.

"Better see what those two dancers look like," Mickey said, and swung his way through the doors. Zander took a moment to clean out his locker. Other than gear there wasn't much, he closed the door, shoving things into his duffle.

Even though there weren't that many people in the gym, Zander put his boot in front of the locker room doors to prevent them from being opened. He lifted the handle of the payphone hanging on the wall next to the doors and dialed the operator.

"How may I assist your call?"

"I need to make a collect call," Zander responded.

"Go ahead sir," said the operator.

Zander gave the faceless woman the number he had memorized, a number he hadn't thought of calling for a long time. He closed his eyes as the ringing began. At the second ring, Zander heard a voice he'd recognize anywhere. "Hello—"

The operator cut in, "I'm calling with a collect call from Reins. Will you accept the charges?"

"Yes, yes of course," said the person on the other end of the line.

Zander heard the click of the call being patched through.

"Zander, is that you?" There was a moment, a pause, and Zander felt relief.

"I'm coming home," he said gruffly. He moved the phone away from his ear and hesitated, but then put the receiver down in the cradle. He picked up his bags and headed for the door. He stopped in front of Bruce to give a quick nod, and then pushed through the gym doors for the last time and headed to the bus station.

Some of the people at the bus station were milling around stretching their legs before having to sit for an extended period of time, others sat wide-awake, waiting for their boarding announcement, while others dozed. Zander leaned against a wall, watching his surroundings. He was waiting for a specific time, 5:30 a.m. Zander had bought a one-way ticket with cash to the half-way point, then he'd switch modes of travel and figure out the rest as he made his way. Once the large hand on the clock clicked into place, Zander turned his attention to the row of payphones he stood near. Sliding his bags over the tiled floor and under a phone, he took some change from his pocket, plunked the coins into the slot, and dialed another familiar number. On the fourth ring, he heard the voice of Mr. Rupert Thayer. "Mr. Thayer here." Zander could imagine Mr. Thayer in the kitchen enjoying his breakfast, reading the newspaper, and completing the crossword before starting the rest of his day.

"Mr. Thayer, it's Zander Blake." Zander faced outward, making sure no one was hovering near him.

"Zander? Well, it's been awhile. How are you?" asked Rupert.

"Mr. Thayer, I'm sorry to bother you. I need to tell you that you might be getting a visit from the Easton police," Zander stated.

"Zander are you alright?" asked Rupert.

"I don't want to get you involved, you and Mrs. Thayer did so much for me. I hope you know how much I appreciate the both of you. I owe it to you to let you know there may be some questions being asked about me." Zander hated having to say this to Mr. Thayer, a man he both admired and respected.

"It's been some time since trouble came to this doorstep," Rupert said jokingly. There was a pause. "Zander, I think the world of you. So did Mrs. Thayer. Whatever has happened, just make sure you're making the right decision," Rupert continued.

"I'm making a decision. Thank you, sir, for everything." Zander hung up the phone slid his bags with his foot back away from the phone bank and stood up against the wall again. He stared at the clock.

There was another person he had to call. He'd not only involve them, but they would have to take a risk. Zander's hand rested on the payphone's receiver. He had run through every option he could think of to keep them out of it, but there was no option that would work without them being involved. He picked up the phone, plunked in the coins, and dialed. It was very early in the morning, and Zander hoped Brad would be lucid enough to understand what Zander needed from him.

"Hello?" Brad answered the phone.

Zander was amazed at how awake Brad sounded. "Brad, it's Zander. Sorry to wake you."

"Ah you didn't wake me; I've been up trying to type this paper. You okay?"

"I need to ask you for a favor."

"Anything, shoot."

"I need you to say you forgot to mark down mileage on the van. Like two hundred eighty miles."

"Okay," Brad responded.

Zander paused at Brad's response. Eventually he repeated, "Okay?"

"Yeah, okay. I mean, I probably did forget to log a trip or two. Wouldn't be the first time," Brad responded.

Zander wanted to stress the seriousness of the situation without giving Brad more information that could make him legally accountable. "Brad, I need you to listen and understand. Something happened last night that is forcing me to leave, and I won't be back. What I'm asking you could lead to implications for you. I want you to know you're not just covering mileage."

"I am listening, and I do understand Zander. Let me ask you something," Brad responded.

"Hmmmm," Zander mumbled, turning to look at the other waiting passengers in the bus terminal. No one was paying any attention to him.

"Whatever it is that happened, would you do it for me if the situation were reversed?" Brad asked.

"Without a doubt."

"Well alright then. Forgotten mileage, done. You need anything else?" Brad asked.

"No. Best not to mention my name to anyone though," Zander added.

"Not even her?" Brad asked.

Zander's eyes snapped closed as he remembered his mouth on hers. "To anyone," Zander responded.

"Okay, Zander," Brad replied.

There was silence. During the summers Zander stayed at the Academy, with Brad in the next town over they had spent lazy afternoons together riding their bikes, fishing, swimming—their whole lives ahead of them. When Zander moved to the city, they kept in touch. Brad had gotten Zander the job at Farm & Pharma. He was the closest thing to a brother Zander had ever had.

"Brad, you take care of yourself. I wish you and Sonny the best," Zander said in a hushed voice.

"Man, Zander, our paths might cross again, you never know. Besides you're the one who sounds like you need to take care of yourself. And I know you know how to. Hey, if you need anything else, man, you know where I am," Brad said.

Zander hung up the phone. The intercom blared; Zander's bus was now boarding. He picked up his bags and headed to the bus platform.

Rupert Thayer hung up the phone. He had thirteen more clues to complete on the crossword. It would have to wait. He finished eating his oatmeal standing up. He cleared the dishes from the table and carried them over to the sink. He looked out at the frost on the ground, covering the remains of the garden. As he mindlessly washed his breakfast dishes, he imagined Natalie snipping flowers here and there to put around the house. She'd be wearing her large straw hat and her gloves, but still her roses would snag on something.

"Well, Natalie, I know what you would say: 'If we can help him,' so that's just what we're going to do." He finished washing his dishes and put them in the dish rack. He tightened his bathrobe belt and headed up the stairs to shower, shave, and dress. He'd be going over to the Admissions building today. He hadn't been in that building for a year, but he was on a mission. Through the bathroom window, the sun's rays hit his eyes. He took it as a sign that Natalie approved of his plan. He pulled the shower curtain closed.

After boarding the bus and finding a seat, Zander made a makeshift pillow with his jacket and slunk down a bit in his seat. He folded his arms over his chest and settled in for the long ride. At first, he looked out the window, watching the familiar city streets go by, then the scenery turned into woods, then mown fields and cornstalks still standing for just a few more weeks. The sun's rays illuminated the day before him. His mind should've been planning what to do after the hours of miles ahead of him ended, or maybe even to Kit, or what he had done, but his thoughts weren't on those. Instead, he thought of her. He may never know if she was alright, he most likely would never see her again, and yet he found himself imagining her, his mind returning to those brief moments with her . . . the softness of her lips, the color in her cheeks. He imagined her with him, their fingers entwined, walking toward a tree line with a fieldstone foundation.

"Now, where is that vest, Natalie?" Rupert Thayer
stood in front of the closet in the hallway by the front
door. He was moving hangers from left to right and then
back again. He was looking specifically for a particular
vest usually used in duck or pheasant hunting with a
large inside pocket for storing maps, shells, a hat, and so
on. With the chill in the air, Rupert would not look at all
suspicious with a vest on. He stood there for a moment
looking in the closet. He didn't see the oatmeal-colored
vest anywhere among the items hanging before him.
Then there was a swift movement, and the vest fell off
one of the wooden hangers to the floor. "Thank you,
Nat, right in front of me, as per usual."

Rupert bent down, grabbed the vest off the floor,
and pulled it on. There, inside on the right, was the

large inside pocket. He felt around inside, it was empty and roomy. "Perfect," Rupert said, straightening the collar, and then grabbed his keys and headed out into the morning sun just as he heard the grandfather clock chime 7:30 a.m.

He made his way across the quad and up to the Admissions building. He knew Lottie would be there early. She had been the secretary at the Academy for years and she had always been early. These days she arrived by the one bus that still ran for the time being between the city, Weston, and Easton. A few years ago, her old car had finally died, and she did not have the resources to get another one. It was just her and her daughter, who worked part time while going to Cosmetology school, and there just wasn't anything to spare for a car. Rupert opened the wooden door leading into the main hall. There she was, Lottie, straightening some papers that had been left on her desk by the teachers the night before.

"Well, as I live and breathe! Mr. Thayer!" Ms. Turner gushed.

"Good morning, Lottie. How have you been?" Rupert asked.

"Oh, just fine, just fine. What are you doing up here?" Lottie asked.

"Just thought I'd poke around. Interested in the new machines you've got upstairs," Rupert lied.

"Oh, I hope they don't think about getting me one of those things. They are so bulky and noisy—beeping at you when you turn it on or when you enter something wrong and when you turn them off! I'll stick to my typewriter and my handwriting, thank you very much," Lottie said matter-of-factly.

"Well, the times are changing," Rupert stated.

"For good or bad," Lottie stated.

"Only time will tell," Rupert agreed.

"Well, I can take you upstairs to where they're inputting all the records. They've been bringing files over from the old record house all this week. I can't attest to the clutter or the dusty, musty smell in that room," Lottie was coming around the corner of her desk, smiling. "How are things with you?" she asked.

Rupert remembered he, Natalie, and Lottie all working at the Academy together, for years. They were young together, and now only Rupert and Lottie were old together. "Oh, I get along, as you do. How's your daughter?"

"Clever she is. One more course and it looks like she'll graduate at the top of her beauty school," praised Lottie.

"That's fantastic, Lottie. She always has such an easy way about her, which puts you at ease when you're talking with her," complimented Rupert.

"She does have that way about her," Lottie agreed.

"Like her mother," Rupert said.

"Oh, thank you Rupert, such a dear to say that. But don't tell her. You know these girls don't want to be anything like their mamas!" They both laughed.

Lottie and Rupert were standing outside the old admissions room. Rupert went to turn the knob to open the door for Lottie, but the door was locked.

"Here, I have the key. With all the equipment we have to lock up everything like Fort Knox now."

Lottie pulled out her ring of keys, slid a shiny new silver one into the lock, and twisted it. She opened the door and turned on the lights. "Well, I'll just turn these on to get them warmed up for the data entry people. Can you imagine, that's their profession?" Lottie went around the room, pushing the buttons of the monitors and clicking over switches for the modems on the large machines that each took up a whole table. They sprang to life with blinking cursors and multiple beeps.

"You're right, Lottie. Very noisy," Rupert observed.

"Once warmed up they'll be quiet. But then the data people come in and all you hear when this door is open are the clicks and clacks of their fingers on those keys. The worst is this one," Lottie moved to a side table where a dark grey machine sat with paper coming out of its back. She clicked that one on, and Rupert could not describe the annoying noise that he heard. All he could gather was that it sounded unhealthy. A cursor moved back and forth rapidly from one end of the green-and-white-striped paper that came out the back. The writing left behind was the date, time, and the crest of the academy, all made up of dots and dashes.

"Lord, but isn't that something?" Rupert said, pointing to the crest.

"It is clever," Lottie concurred.

Rupert stood up and looked around the room. How much it had changed since his days as headmaster. He saw all of the boxes holding old school records piled on top of one another. His eyes followed the years written on their sides.

"How far along are they with their entries?" Rupert asked.

"They've made it to the eighties. Seriously, the eighties! The fingers on those data people are fast. They stop for half-an-hour lunch, which from what I can gather is made up of chips and soda, and then back at it they go." Lottie looked at her watch. "They'll be in any minute now. I'd better get moving. You look around. I'm sure if you want you could stay and watch the data-entry process. I'm sure they wouldn't mind, probably wouldn't even notice you," she turned to the door, stopping at the frame. "It's really good to see you, Rupert. Don't be a stranger," and then she was gone, turning on lights, starting the coffee pots, and getting ready to start the school day.

Rupert, hearing Lottie's heels go down the stairs, turned quickly to the boxes before him. "Ok, 1980s . . . he was in the class of, so it would be in—" he moved around the boxes, eyeing the years printed on their sides. "Bingo—this one!" It was sandwiched between two other boxes. He lifted the top one off carefully, getting a good whiff of musty smell. He placed it on the floor by his feet, then he turned to the one he needed. He listened for a moment and heard nothing but the whirring of the machines that surrounded him. He flung off the lid and began flicking through the manila folders lined up inside. The files were arranged like the boys on their graduation day waiting for their names to be called. "Adams, Albert, Baker, Berne, Blake—Got it," he pulled out Zander's folder. There, paper clipped to the front, was the picture of the young boy he and Nat were so fond of. Rupert pushed the files together in the box to conceal the empty slot, then replaced the lid and put the other box back on top of it. He went to the doorway and listened again. Still quiet. He slid the thin folder into the inner pocket of his vest, then went out into the hall and down the stairs.

Lottie turned to him, "You're not staying to see the production of the chronology?"

"Nah, too noisy. I don't see what all the fuss is about. Thanks for showing it to me. You take care of yourself, Lottie, and good luck to your daughter," Rupert said as he went to the front door.

"Take care, Rupert," Lottie called after him.

Rupert pushed out through the door. He could see the first few cars coming up the long drive to the school. He saw the first one stop at the guard shack and be waved on through by the guard. Rupert made his way across the quad to home. He climbed up on the porch and the porch swing moved a bit, yet there was no breeze. He turned to the porch swing. "I did it, Nat." he patted the pocket holding the concealed folder. "I got it."

Zander shifted in his seat. When the bus stopped, he'd take his backpack and go outside to walk around and stretch. Time seemed to slow for Zander. He sensed a pull, a pull coming from the direction from which he was running. At each station where he stretched, he eyed the payphones. He could call, he could call the hospital and make sure she was okay, but he knew he couldn't, and he turned from the temptation each time.

Emil placed the receiver back in its cradle and sighed. He remembered the last time he had seen Zander, the day he had sent him away. Emil then remembered the angry words Zander had spoken to him, ones Emil carried with him every day, hoping he had made the right choice by the boy. Emil turned to the bookcase where, on the top shelf, were photos of Emil and his family and friends. He reached for a photo. It was of Emil, Zander, Geoffrey Blake—Zander's grandfather, and Zander's parents—Jacob and Klara Blake. As he looked over the photos, he spoke. "He said he would never come back." Emil hesitated, then he put the picture down and looked out the window toward the tree line where the pipeline ran along. Something was wrong. He noticed the trees had begun to move, yet it was a calm day.

Emil's dog, Mishka, came over to his side. He reached down and patted the faithful companion on the head. Then he turned and went into his bedroom. In the bottom dresser drawer was a stack of papers in an envelope with a green logo on it of a scale with a bird and tree on one side and a stack of coins on the other. He took them out and flipped through them until he found the one he was looking for. Emil took the letter with him back to the phone and dialed the number at the bottom of the letter, a number he hadn't thought of in some time.

"Thank you for calling the Universal Supply Companies and Holdings. How may I assist you?" The woman who answered had an upper crust accent.

"I need to speak directly to the CEO. This is Emil Attla from the Trans-Atlantic Pipeline outfit."

There was a pause on the other end, then her voice came back on the line. "Of course, sir. Please hold the line while I connect you."

"Thank you," Emil responded.

"You're very welcome, sir," she replied.

Emil heard another slight pause and then nothing until he heard the familiar voice of the man who had been involved in the pipeline from its inception. Many years ago, the man had visited the state of Alaska and travelled through its vast wilderness. He had taken Emil, Geoffrey, and Jacob under his wing. When placed in command of the operations in Emil's borough, he tried hard to placate all parties when it came to the finalization of the pipe's placement. Charlie Jewett was fascinated with the culture and the wilderness he was surrounded by and wanted to preserve as much of it as he could. He had a home built up in the mountains that he hoped to go back to one day, his health permitting. It had been years since he had been up in that wild country air. "Policies and bureaucratic bullshit," as he was so fond of saying, had kept him from enjoying much of this one life he had. But he refused to let go of the power. When his personal phone line lit up, he was curious, as that light hadn't blinked at him for many weeks.

When his business on the pipeline ended, he was needed back in the office thousands of miles away. He kept in touch with several people in Alaska whom he thought of as more than just business relationships. But soon their lives took off to raising families, work, education, and travel. The letters and phone calls turned into an occasional birthday or holiday card, then to silence. He picked up the phone. "Yes."

"Mr. Jewett, I have a Mr. Emil Attla on the line for you," said the woman in her crisp accent.

Charlie sat up abruptly and with a rush of words said, "Well, put him through then!" He heard the line connect and didn't hesitate, "Emil? Is it really you?"

"Hello, Charlie. It is," replied Emil.

"It's been ages! So good to hear your voice, it hasn't changed. How have you been?" Charlie rushed.

"I've been well, Charlie. Wondering when you will be back in these parts?"

"Good to hear. I would be there tomorrow if I could."

"Well, then, do it man! No time like the present. I've been looking in on the place, all has been well. A few trees came down this past spring, my boy Chip and I removed them," Emil said.

"Chip? I've never met him," Charlie replied, trying to picture a face with the name.

"No, he was born after you left."

"I'd love to meet him," Charlie said.

"And you will once you come back up here. He actually works on the pipe, so he's one of your boys now." The men shared a chuckle.

"Oh, Emil it's so good to hear from you. Still the snow and mud? Still the coffee klatch at the General Store?" Charlie asked.

"Always to all of the above, not much has changed. Look Charlie, I'm calling with a purpose," Emil knew he had to get to the point.

"Well, let's have it," Charlie said in his business-like tone and sat back in his leather chair.

"Jacob Blake's boy, Zander, he called me," Emil stated.

"Where's he been?" Charlie knew both names, and their faces haunted him.

"I'm not sure. He said he's coming home," Emil replied.

"After all this time?" asked Charlie.

"I don't know anything else, but the day was calm and now the wind has picked up and Mishka is restless," Emil stated as he watched Mishka pace between him and the window. "I'm not sure what the boy will need, but I feel responsible for him still," said Emil.

"There's an opening on the pipe. A pipe boy position where you are. I'll make it happen." Charlie had flipped open a folder that held the list of openings on the pipe. "At least he'll have an income. What else are you sensing Emil?" Charlie asked as he scribbled notes on a piece of paper.

"I'm not sure yet. I think it's best if we roll him into the fold as Zander Reins. Get him some new documents," Emil stated.

"I'll take care of it, Emil. I want you to know I, too, feel responsible for the boy. My priorities when the tragedy happened were not what they should've been. I did a real disservice to that boy and his family. It has weighed on me through the years. Whatever I can do to help, do not hesitate to contact me," Charlie said, sitting up. His elbows rested on top of his large, impressive desk.

"We both know at our age we don't have time to not make this right. Once he arrives, I'll find out more. If I need anything I'll let you know," Emil confirmed.

"You should let me know straight away if we are up against anything. I can mount a better defense if we have time on our side," Charlie replied.

"I will, Charlie. Thank you for this," Emil said.

"I'll wait to hear from you, Emil," Charlie said, and then hung up the phone.

Emil hung up the phone, then knelt down and ruffled Mishka's fur. "Once he arrives it will settle," Emil said, attempting to reassure. Him or the dog, he wasn't sure which. He looked out the window at the wind blowing the aspens, furiously stripping them of their final leaves. "And then another kind of unsettled will begin."

Charlie, leaving the receiver for a moment in its cradle, looked at one of the few photos on his desk. The frame held a picture of Emil, Geoffrey, Jacob, and Charlie. At their feet was a young Zander. The men had their arms on each other's shoulders, on one side of the foursome was a milepost marker—4-4-2. Charlie thought back to all the hard work they had done. The long hours and trying days, the endless red tape and bureaucracy they faced each day, the incidents all along the way, the accidents, the deaths. The deaths. Charlie and Emil and some of the local law enforcement officers were the ones to find Jacob, Zander's father, and another man, or what was left of them after the wolves got to them. And then the fire and the deaths of Geoffrey and Klara, leaving Zander an orphan. Those weren't the only issues Charlie had dealt with on the company side. There were deadlines to meet, there was money to be made. "Not just our ages, Emil," Charlie said, still looking at the photograph. "But with our health. My health," Charlie paused, "I need to make this right." Charlie picked up the phone and was automatically connected to his secretary. "Margene, get me Rhoda in personnel. Tell her to come see me immediately."

"Yes, Mr. Jewett," Margene replied.

He put the receiver down, leaning his elbows on the desk. He looked at a silver frame holding the picture of a young girl with glossy chestnut brown hair and olive skin. Her champion horse stood behind her with its head leaning over the girl's shoulder. "Yes, at our age we can't waste any more time," Charlie said.

Zander had made it to the halfway point of his trip. He was relieved to get off the bus and stop moving for a bit. He walked around the bus station, trying to get his bearings. He looked at the bus map hanging on the bus station wall. He swung his backpack over his shoulder, and carrying his duffle bag, he pushed through the glass door of the bus station and went out onto the sidewalk. The air was crisp in this mountain town, mixed in was the smell of food. There was a diner strategically located right next to the bus station. "Open twenty-four hours," the sign boasted. He could do with a cup of coffee. He went up the three steps to the one-story whitewood-sided building and pushed through the door. A bell rang over his head. To his left and right were booths original to the 1950s structure. In them sat patrons enjoying their meals. The linoleum counter was before him and ran the length of the building, and in front of it swivel barstools with fake leather padding were bolted to the floor. There was a break at the end of the counter for the waitress to go back and forth from the kitchen to the dining area. To the far right were the restrooms.

"Hey there, hon. You can sit anywhere you like, and I'll be right with you," a tall, busty woman called from behind the counter. She was busy lining up plates along her wide arm to carry over to a family sitting in a booth. Zander nodded and headed for the end of the counter, to an empty barstool away from others and the door in plain sight. By the time Zander had tucked his bags under the counter and sat down, the waitress was before him. She flipped over the coffee cup on the little saucer that she had set in front of him. "Coffee, luv?" she asked.

"Hmmm," Zander replied and nodded.

"Here's some cream and sugar. I'll be back for your order," she replied.

"Just coffee is fine," Zander replied.

His words caught in his throat. He hadn't spoken to anyone for several states. He cleared his throat. She turned to him. "You don't look like you live on just coffee. Look over the menu, the turkey special is really good. You should try that," she said with a wink.

"Fine," Zander didn't hesitate. He didn't want to argue, he didn't want a fuss over him. He ran his hands over his thighs and looked toward the door as the bell chimed. A couple came through the door of the diner laughing about something. They must've been regulars because they didn't wait to be told to take a seat. They walked together to the last open booth on the left wall.

"There, now. See, that wasn't so hard," the waitress said as she took the menu away and popped the order slip into a rotating metal wheel for the kitchen staff to deal with. Zander kept telling himself to relax, to not be noticeable, and, looking around the crowded diner, he thought he'd slip by and just be one of the forgotten faces that passed through here. He reached for the cup of coffee and took a sip, then put the cup back in its saucer. He pulled in a deep breath as he rested his arms on the counter and leaned over his space. His eyes looked into the darkness of the coffee.

When the local station got ahold of the story, the residents of Easton were rattled. The name of the deceased and the other victim wasn't released, but in small towns there's no such thing as a secret. It didn't help that the police cruisers were stacked in Waverly Germaine's driveway for all traveling that road on their way into or out of town to see.

As Waverly Germaine lay in a hospital bed and the body of Kit Mayfield, son of Harold and Kathleen Mayfield, lay in the morgue, Brad and Sonny heard the news over the local radio station. Brad kept repeating it over and over, *Forgotten mileage, remember the forgotten mileage.* Mr. Thayer, having returned from the academy to the inside of his house, decided to head into Easton to pick up some groceries. At the covered bridge, the radio broadcast that there had been an attack, and instead of taking the straight road into Easton, something pulled him to go to the left, the long way, the way he used to go each Friday night. He slowed when he reached the beginning of the Germaine's property. At the stone wall, he could already see police cruisers on the ridge and a white pickup truck. He faced forward and made his way to town. At the Town Green, he maneuvered his car through streets that held more than the usual number of people. The crowds were gathered around the park benches and the gazebo, and there were quite a few people standing on the steps to the police station. Mr. Thayer thought back to the phone call he'd received that morning and wondered if the commotion was related. He took a left, heading out of town. There, a little way past the storefronts, the street turned to older homes with sprawling porches, and up on the hill sat the hospital. Rupert had driven this way for many months a few years ago, and he was not looking forward to driving up the hill to the visitor's parking lot and going through those wide sliding doors. But he had a sinking feeling, and he knew it had to be done.

He parked the car in a spot very close to the one he had last parked in years before. After exiting his car, he pushed the door closed and looked at his reflection. She wasn't in there, he knew that. Natalie had died a while ago. Now he needed to see if someone else near and dear to him was in the hospital. He turned away from his car and walked to the entrance and through the doors. At the information desk say Peggy Bluet, part of a long-time family of Easton and a friend of Natalie's.

"Oh Rupert, I'm so glad you're here. They brought in Waverly this morning. She looked a fright. The police are with her now. The gift shop just opened. They have a lovely batch of lilies, I'm sure she'd like those. Oh Rupert, it's just terrible. I'm so glad you're here. Room 107," she blurted out.

With Peggy there was no such thing as confidentiality, not to a fellow Eastoner. Rupert had no problem asking her questions. "Why are the police with her?"

"She was attacked. In her very own house! No one is safe anymore. We were such a quiet town and now, well, if it can happen to such a sweet girl like Waverly, well . . . you know I'll be locking my doors for sure from now on," replied Peggy.

"I'd better head up and see her," Rupert stated, heading for the corridor.

"You go on now. So good of you to come, Rupert. She has no one," Peggy said forlornly.

Rupert went to the gift shop and picked out the hydrangeas for Waverly he knew she'd like those more than the lilies that Peggy had suggested. He found himself miffed at what Peggy had said, that Waverly had no one. She had him, and Miriam Stetter, and he was sure she had friends. Rupert paid for the flowers and headed to room 107. He knew the hospital very well. He had spent much time here with Natalie. Even though it was a smaller hospital than the one in the city, it offered many of the same treatments and procedures.

Chief Jebidiah Hayden and an officer stood outside of Waverly's room. Their backs were to Rupert, and even though they spoke in a hushed tone, their words echoed down the corridor. Rupert could make out what Chief Hayden was saying. "We've got one dead body, a busted-up female, and an unknown male assailant. Mr. Mayfield has been riding me like one of his racehorses. We've got to figure this out. You head back to the crime scene and make sure everything is being done correctly. I'm going to head on over to the head doc and see if he can be available to see her when she wakes up." Chief Hayden turned, looking into the room. From the corner of his eye, he caught something and turned. Standing beside him was Rupert Thayer. "Oh, hey there Rupert. How are you?" Chief Hayden asked.

"I'm fine, Jeb. Heard there's been a commotion," Rupert replied.

"Well, I can't say anything officially, but I can tell you we have it all under control."

"That's reassuring to hear," Rupert said, thinking, *Yeah right.* "If you don't mind, I'm just going to go in and visit Waverly for a bit," Rupert stated.

"She's sleeping. Hasn't woken up since the ER when they did x-rays. She's a tough girl, that one," said Chief Hayden.

The officers stepped aside, and Rupert took a deep breath and walked into the room. He saw Waverly lying in the hospital bed. He had seen her get tossed from horses while riding, fall out of a tree house, and fall off of bikes, but seeing her there in that bed, she seemed so small and, for a brief moment, he saw Natalie laying in that bed. He put the flowers in the vase on the side table and pulled a chair over to the side of the bed. He looked to the open door. Chief Hayden and the officer were gone.

"Hey there, kiddo. It's Rupert, Mr. Thayer. Just came by to see you," Rupert lifted her hand and held it in his, then he rubbed her hand with his thumb. The beeping of the monitor and the whirling noise of some other machine were in the background.

"Oh, my sweet girl. You will be alright," his voiced cracked a bit, and he wasn't sure if he was saying that to convince himself or her. He looked at her. The right side of her face was bruised, a deep purple and black. He winced. She seemed to be resting peacefully, which he knew she needed. He rose from his chair, bent over her quietly, and kissed her forehead lightly. "Sleep, my dear. I will be seeing you soon." He righted himself and quietly walked to the door where he turned briefly, looking back on the young woman he had seen mature from a curious little girl. Then he left, heading for the exit and his car.

Peggy had to get another word in. "A pity, such a tragedy for this town. I'm so glad Waverly isn't worse. I mean poor Kit, and Harold and Kathleen must be distraught."

Rupert stopped in his tracks. "What about Kit?" he asked, turning to Peggy.

She lowered her voice and whispered, "He was found dead in her house, beaten to death. Imagine after being missing for months and then to be found dead. I can't imagine what Kathleen and Harold are going through."

"I hope you never do," Rupert said. The sliding glass doors opened for him, and he walked toward his car. Once seated behind the wheel with the door closed, he thought of the phone call from Zander in the early morning.

Zander knew he couldn't swallow any food. His stomach had gone from knots to rusted chain as the reality of what he had done sunk in. He reached for the coffee cup, and noticed his hand and his knuckles were still pretty banged up. He quickly put his left hand in his lap. He looked around at the other patrons in the diner. All were busy talking with their eating companions or getting up to leave and continue their day. No one had taken notice of him. He sat there for a moment, knowing he couldn't live like this, always looking over his shoulder. The door swung open again and Zander's eyes snapped to the movement. In came an old man, wearing multiple layers, a buildup of grime on his face. The waitress greeted him. "Hey there, Dusty. You have enough for coffee?"

"I do, just enough," the man spoke with a gravelly voice, came over to the counter, and selected a stool not far from Zander. He pulled a handful of coins from his pocket and let them fall on the countertop. The coins swiveled and turned, making clinking noises as they settled flat. The man began counting from the largest coin denomination, but soon found himself counting out pennies. Zander watched as the waitress brought over the turkey special and plunked the platter down in front of Zander.

She turned to Dusty, saying, "Not sure you pan-handled enough there, hon."

Zander couldn't even stomach the smell of the food in front of him. With a sweeter tone she turned back to Zander. "It comes with either peach cobbler or lemon meringue pie."

Zander noticed that when peach cobbler was mentioned, Dusty's eyes looked toward the dessert tray. "Peach cobbler," Zander said.

"Sure thing, luv." She swayed her hips over to the dessert caddy and removed a pre-sliced piece of cobbler. Zander meanwhile was taking out his wallet. He pulled a hundred-dollar bill from it and got up from the barstool. He grabbed his duffle and backpack in one hand, sliding the turkey platter with the other in front of Dusty who was coming up three cents short of a cup of coffee. Zander slid the hundred bill under the platter. "Enjoy, man," Zander said. To the waitress, who stood there dumbstruck, Zander said, "You can set that right there," indicating Dusty's stool.

"Thank you, sir," Dusty said to Zander.

Zander moved to the door and, as the bell chimed above his ears, he gave a sideways glance back at Dusty sitting at the counter, eating probably the first real meal he had in days.

In the dusky evening, the streetlights of the town were just beginning to come on. Zander looked to the fuel station across the way, several big rigs parked outside. That would be his best bet. He crossed the two-lane street and went up to the glass door with a metal bar to push it open with. Through it, he could see a gathering of truckers. Some perused the aisles for snacks, others filled up their large coffee thermoses for the road. As Zander walked through the door, he heard the tones of familiarity. These men had run into one another here before, or elsewhere on the open highway.

Zander went up and down a few of the aisles until he found what he was looking for. He grabbed some gauze and first-aid cream from the shelf and carried them up to the register. Once he paid, he headed to the restroom where he found himself in a stall, raising his shirt and looking at the black line on his side. He bandaged himself up and headed back out to see if he could hitch a ride for the next, and last, leg of his journey.

Zander saw one older man wearing a hat with the state of Alaska embroidered on it, a flannel shirt, and jeans that were held up with a belt and large belt buckle with a bison engraved on it. This man was slight in stature, possibly in his late sixties or early seventies. He was filling up his thermos and keeping to himself, yet the other men near him nodded to him. This was the man Zander approached, a seasoned trucker.

"You heading to the Yukon by any chance?" asked Zander.

The man turned to look at Zander, taking him and his duffle bag in. "Yeah, I travel them roads," he responded.

"Are you opposed to a traveler?"

"That's a fair piece to have a stowaway." The man used the truckers' term for a hitchhiker, and a few others turned slightly to where the old man and Zander stood.

"I'd be looking to go the miles until right below the first mountain crest."

"I got no frills in my rig, no time for nonsense either," he said as he twisted the cap onto his thermos.

"You got a co-pilot chair?" Zander asked.

"That I do," the man said with a chuckle. "Alright then, let's go."

The men walked out into the dusk toward a shiny black rig with a silver bullet behind it. The two men climbed up into the cab on their respective sides. The trucker directed Zander to throw his stuff in the back.

"So, you looking for work up there? Back when the pipe was being built, there was more work for anyone. Now, it's a bit tough," he said as he turned the ignition over.

"What should I call you?" asked Zander, changing the topic. He settled into the co-pilot's chair.

"Westie."

Zander nodded.

"I only work west of the Rockies; you won't see me doing the latters," he continued, meaning the lateral highways that crossed the country. "I like the ups and downs on this side of the mountain range. And what should I call you?" Westie asked, turning to look at Zander.

"Zander."

The big rig pulled out of the parking lot just as the neon light of the diner came on. Westie turned the wheels with ease, heading north. Zander settled in, watching the outlying buildings pass by. He folded his arms across his chest and sighed.

"So, what are you looking for up there?" asked Westie.

"Redemption."

Zander's file had been moved around the house wherever Rupert situated himself. He didn't let it out of his sight, but there was no word from Zander. With every phone call his heart leapt, sifting through the mail he expected to find a clue, but there was none. Finally, one morning he went to the front parlor to his fine, impressive desk with carved feet in the shape of lion's paws, he unlocked a drawer, and slid in Zander's file. A reflection bounced across the desk through the windows and flashed in Rupert's eyes. He held open a curtain to see Harold Mayfield's white pickup truck coming up the drive to the Academy, turning toward Rupert's house. He let the curtain go as he turned the desk key in its lock and slid it into the pocket of his slacks.

Once outside the city's limits, Westie settled in. He set the speed, the music station for the ride, and lit up the CB radio by doing call outs to the rigs passing by.

When the night darkness was over the road before them, Zander spoke. "How long have you been driving?" he asked.

"Oh, after I lived through the war, got out of the service, and just couldn't settle down. Decided to keep moving."

"You must've seen a lot over the years, changes in the landscape."

"Oh yeah, and changes in the people too. People aren't what they used to be."

"Hmmm," Zander agreed.

"I've seen this road turn on you through the seasons.

A month or two from now, you better have your wits about you when you drive her. Sun shining one minute and a whiteout the next. You can't run from what ails you, son. Because that's just it, it's what ails you," Westie emphasized the *you*, with a glance at Zander.

Zander rested his hands on his thighs as he leaned back in his seat. Mile after mile the two men talked, mostly Westie, of this and that, not spending too much time on any given topic. Westie had the timing between stops for his rig down to a science. Zander got out and stretched his legs, took a glance at the newspapers and their headlines, milled around the payphones, and Westie watched him with curiosity. *For someone who doesn't say much, he sure hovers around phones, as if he has a lot to say,* Westie thought. He noticed that the young man was jumpy, uneasy, and looked behind him every so often. But once back inside the cab and on the road, he seemed to relax just a bit. Westie headed into his bunk for his timed sleep and Zander put his seat back and stared out the window, sitting with his thoughts running wild. He thought of Kit lying there on the floor. He thought of Waverly in her barn. He thought of when she had her hand on his side, the look of concentration on her face as she stitched him up. He thought of her mouth.

It had been a little over a week, since Zander had joined Westie on the road. They were making good time; the men's journey together was coming to an end. Zander recognized the road that Westie had pulled onto after clearing the last border. Soon Zander would have to face Emil and places he thought he had put behind him.

Rupert opened the door just as Harold Mayfield was starting to climb the steps of the porch.

"Well, good morning, Rupert."

"Morning Harold. What brings you here to the Academy?"

"Not here for the Academy. Here to talk with you."

"Oh, about what?" Rupert asked.

"Well, I'm sure you've heard of the death of my son, Kit."

"Yes."

Harold Mayfield looked around then looked up at Rupert standing stoically on the porch. "You know, most people would say their condolences to a grieving father."

"I didn't realize you were here because you were grieving Harold. I am sorry though for Kathleen, to lose a child is I'm sure a very painful loss."

"He was my son too you know."

The men had reached a standoff, after a bit Harold broke the silence. "You know, most people would also invite a friend in."

"Harold, we were never what you would call friends. What is it that brings you here?"

"You were always straight to the point Rupert. Fine, I need information on a student of yours. That Zander Blake character you had here a few years ago, the same one who tried to pin the break-in to Lenny's store on Kit." Rupert tilted his head holding Harold's gaze. "C'mon Rupert you know who I mean, and I need answers! My boy is about to be rotting in his grave because that scum held a grudge against my boy and killed him. Now who is he and where can I find him?"

"You could go up to the admissions building and ask those questions, but I'm sure Chief Hayden will get all those answers for you, as I know you two are what you would call, friends."

Rupert turned his back to Harold. While opening the door to his house, he said over his shoulder, "You take care now Harold, go home. Be with Kathleen."

The straight and wide came into view as Westie pulled the rig onto the street. Zander noticed there were a few new, sleek buildings that didn't seem to quite fit in with the rest of town, but for the most part the buildings were all the same. He saw the road leading out of town and hoped for a second that Westie would just keep his foot down and continue on, but the rig was slowly rolling to a stop.

"Well, you made it," Westie said. "I'm gonna head over there for a bit."

Zander followed Westie's eyes, looking in the direction of the General Store. Lined up along the straight and wide were other big rigs like Westie's, and Zander knew their owners or drivers were inside, gathered around the old Hoosier cabinet in the back, talking and drinking coffee. The two exited the rig. Zander carried his duffle in one hand, his backpack slung over his shoulder.

Zander held out a hand. "I thank you for taking me along. I appreciate it."

"You find yourself without work, you just let me know. There's always room for another road warrior. I think you'd fit right in," Westie replied, shaking Zander's hand firmly.

Westie looked both ways on the straight and wide before crossing. Zander stood on the opposite side of the road looking at the General Store, and then he turned his head to the right. The guns and ammo and the taxidermist store were still there, but the sign had been repainted. There were a couple more bars than he remembered. To his left was a clothing outfitter store, a bank, and a diner. Zander faced the General Store again. Parked alongside the big rigs there were trucks lined up, including one he recognized, a two-door silver Ford. In the bed of the truck stood a husky who was looking right at Zander and had been since Zander had come into sight. Zander crossed the street, heading for the truck and dog. The dog's tail began to wag in recognition. Zander, now next to the truck, dropped his duffel bag on the ground.

"Hey there, girl," Zander said as he reached up slowly. The dog sniffed Zander's hand and then began to rapidly lick it. Zander began to pet and scratch the dog. "It's good to see you, my friend."

Westie went through the door to the General Store. The familiar sleigh bells rang above his head. He looked to the back corner where fellow truckers and some locals were gathered, talking. They turned when the door opened and called out greetings to the known trucker. He called out "Hullo," but before heading toward them he turned to the counter to greet the owners of the General Store and Post Office, but Dika and Patuk were nowhere to be seen. He shuffled to the gathering. One man who had seen almost as many miles as Westie poured him a cup of coffee. "Welcome back. Where'd the journey begin?" he asked as he handed him the cup.

"Oh, just outside Boulder for this leg. Zipped through Valdez. Tomorrow I'll hock a left and see the Northern lights."

Westie took the cup of black coffee and took a sip. It tasted the same as it did every time he came through this town, the same brew, the same company, he knew soon he'd be turning back around and would come through here in a week or so and maybe make one more trip before the pass closed for the season. One big rig owner was looking out at the straight and wide.

"Hey Emil," he said, "Who's that out by your truck?"

The men turned and saw Zander getting much attention from the husky. Westie looked out mid sip of coffee.

"Oh, that was my stowaway. Zander's his name."

Emil had been leaning against the wall, next to an elder with long white hair, grey smoke streaks running through it, who sat in a wooden folding chair. The elder turned to Emil and said, "The wind has settled."

"For now, Quinn," Emil replied.

Emil pushed off the wall and headed to the front door. Patuk and Dika came from the back storeroom, each carrying boxes. Westie turned to the couple, raising his coffee cup to them. "Still the best cup of joe this side of the Rockies."

"Westie how are you?" asked Patuk as he put down his box and went over to shake hands with the familiar trucker. Dika made her way to the front of the store and put her box down on the General Store's counter that ran the length of the wall. As Emil walked by, Dika pulled an envelope from the pigeon slot of mailboxes behind the counter. She held out her arm and, in her hand was the envelope with the familiar green logo. Emil took it with a nod of his head and then headed out the door. Dika watched Emil through the glass as he walked to the man by his truck.

Emil stood beside Zander for a bit watching him get reacquainted with Mishka, the husky. Finally, he spoke. "You have grown into quite a young man," he said to Zander.

"Hmmm," Zander replied.

For a moment, he stopped petting Mishka and turned to Emil. The men looked at one another in silence. Emil held out his hand and Zander saw the man who had taken his family in when they had first arrived in Alaska, had taken him in after the slaughter of his family. And he saw the man who had sent him away to get an education, the man he forgave and was grateful for. He extended his hand, and the men shook and then embraced.

"Let's get you home," said Emil.

Zander picked up his duffel bag and flung it into the bed of the truck. The husky immediately went to it and lay down beside it. Zander went over to the passenger side and climbed in. Emil sat behind the steering wheel. Zander put his backpack at his feet. Once the doors were shut and they were sitting in silence, Emil spoke. "So, are you going to tell me why you've come back now, after all this time?"

Zander looked at the straight and wide heading out of town and to the mountains where he knew Emil's house sat. "How about after a shower?"

"Sounds good." Emil put the truck in reverse and began heading out of town in the direction of the mountain. He lifted his pointer finger from the hand that held the steering wheel, as a wave to those they passed. The dark red leather interior of the truck had a few more scratches in it then Zander recalled, but the smell was the same as he remembered, grease mixed with freshly cut wood.

"As you can see, not much has changed. The pipe boys have a new building. Got a transplant from the Lower 48 working there. Name's William Parkst. Nice man, has a wife. Lives up there in that green house," Emil pointed out toward a side street branching off the straight and wide on Zander's side of the truck. Zander wasn't sure why Emil was telling him about this man William Parkst, but he listened and looked out at the street and caught a glimpse of the house Emil mentioned. "New Lodge too," Emil continued, "that one right there with the glass A-Frame. All of us are proud of that building. It's prominent, as it should be."

"Hmmm," Zander agreed.

When Emil was describing the new building, he should've noted that it was six years old, which he and many of the people in the borough still considered new. Emil decided to press. "Look, I'm not sure if you're staying or what, but I called up Charlie," he stated, removing the envelope that Dika had handed to him before he left the General Store from inside his jacket. He held it out to Zander.

"I got you a job as a pipe boy and new documents, papers."

"Why would you do that?" Zander asked gruffly.

"Do what exactly, Zander? Look out for you the best way I know how? Try to do best by you?" Emil responded harshly.

Zander took the envelope and saw the return address of the pipe company. "I don't want you to think that I don't appreciate all that you have ever done for me Emil, because I do. Without you I don't know what I would've done, but now—I don't know. Maybe I would've been better off . . . ," his voice trailed off.

"What matters is that you're here, you have found your way back. You are back, right?" Emil pressed. His pressing had run out. Zander looked at Emil with an annoyed expression on his face.

"I thought we agreed, after a shower?"

"Fine. Fine," Emil gave a slight smile out of the corner of his mouth as they rode in silence toward the mountain in the distance.

Rupert found himself randomly patting the right front pocket of his slacks, verifying that his desk key was still in its place. The visit from Harold Mayfield put him on edge. He couldn't help wondering what had happened that night involving Zander with Kit's death and Waverly's hospitalization. Rupert stared at the phone in the kitchen, silent in its receiver. He pulled the small stack of envelopes from the entryway table and flipped through them slowly in case he missed something, he hadn't. A car door slammed. Rupert tossed the envelops back on the table. He opened the door fully prepared to tell Harold where he could go but found himself face to face with Chief Jebidiah Hayden.

"Oh, sorry there Mr. Thayer. You heading out?"

"No Jeb, I was just going to enjoy the air for a bit here on the porch with my pipe." Rupert pulled from his toggled sweater cardigan his pipe, tobacco, and matches; he patted the pocket again.

"Well, I really wish this was a social call, but I'm here on official business."

"And what business would that be?" Rupert asked.

"The mess with Waverly Germaine and Kit Mayfield. We have a lead on a suspect, and I have some questions for you."

"Who is 'we'?"

"What?" Jebidiah asked with a confused expression.

"You said 'we' Jeb, who is the 'we' you are talking about?"

"I mean me, and the police station, so, we."

"Ah," Rupert replied.

"Anyway, the suspect is a man named Zander Blake. He went to school here at the Academy, graduated a few years back, nineteen-eighty—"

"You can't expect me to remember all the graduates from the Academy Jeb."

"Er, well no, but this one, he well—"

"I don't see how I can help you Jeb. I can however tell you that the Academy is going through a technology overhaul. They hired a bunch of technicians to enter in all the student records, moved them all from the old record house to the admissions building. If you have the year this Zander person graduated, you could start there."

"Well, that's very helpful Mr. Thayer, thank you, I greatly appreciate it."

Rupert, cool as could be, puffed on his pipe as Chief Hayden walked away with a bounce in his step to his patrol car.

Emil was a guide and a scout, and he knew both the land and the people. He was respected in the community, and when the big bosses of the pipeline came to the town and met with the elders years ago, Emil was included in those meetings. He was chosen to help with the location of the pipeline and was consulted by many of the pipeline investors, including Charlie Jewett, on the placement of the pipe, taking into consideration the concerns of the people, the land, and the animals.

Emil's house stood on a perpetual lease of land that he earned by working for the pipeline. Emil and his friends constructed his home. It was a simple two-story house, painted dark blue, and had a dirt road leading up to it. It sat in a cleared, open space and was surrounded by wooded pines with trails leading off toward the pipeline, which was visible. Zander noticed when Emil's house came into view that not much had changed since he had last seen it. As they exited the truck, Emil put down the tailgate and called for Mishka to get down, but it was not needed, as the dog was already on the ground and pushing into Zander, who was lifting his duffel over the side of the truck. Emil stood for a moment, remembering Zander as a young boy standing almost exactly where he was now, both men and dog younger than they were now. He closed the tailgate and headed for the front door.

In the kitchen, Zander put his duffel and backpack down. He took off his vest and unzipped his hoodie, then he pulled off the layers of clothing, piling them on top of his bags. Emil was getting something out of the fridge, and when he turned, Zander was standing there, leaning up against the sink, looking at his side. Emil looked to where Zander was looking and saw the stitches.

"Those need to be taken out," Emil said.

"Hmmm," Zander mumbled in agreement.

Emil put down the carton of milk and headed to the downstairs bathroom, retrieving a pair of small, sharp shears and a pair of tweezers. He pulled a chair away from the kitchen table and sat in front of Zander. He held the scissors in one hand and the tweezers in the other and leaned in, looking at the stitches. He then leaned back and put the items in one hand, then reached into his shirt front pocket. He removed his glasses from the case and put them on. Zander shook his head and raised his eyebrows, thinking he could just do this himself. Emil leaned in again and raised his hands, then stopped again. Zander dropped his head back, trying to be patient. Emil looked up and said in an annoyed voice, "I suppose I can't ask about these either until after the shower?"

Zander snapped his head forward and looked at Emil, annoyance visible in both men. Emil turned back to the stitches. "Well, whoever did these, they have tight stitching."

Click went the scissors as they snipped the threads one by one, and then the slight tug of the strings. Zander looked out the window opposite him and thought of standing with Waverly in the doorway of her porch.

Finally, with a pull of the last stitch, Emil finished. He rose from his chair, gathered the debris, and put it all in the waste bin. "Everything's where it was. I left your room for you. Make yourself at home. I'll be in the living room waiting for you, after your shower," he said.

He went down the hall and sat in his chair. He rocked a bit and, realizing that his patience was not what it used to be, he picked up a book from the stand next to him and began reading it, hoping to pass the time and distract himself. But Emil's soft brown face showed anything but distraction or interest in the book he was holding. His black eyebrows furrowed over his brown eyes, which had a reddish tint to them, like a red-tailed hawk. His features were sharp and narrow. His thin lips were firmly pressed together. Emil's blue-black hair, which just brushed his shoulders when down, was pulled back in a slight ponytail. Silver strands ran through it, creating a glint when the light hit it.

Zander took a look around; the kitchen was the same, with the breakfast nook holding a wooden table and four matching chairs with seat cushions tied onto their spindles. The linoleum floor was spotless, and the breakfast dishes were drying in the dish rack. Mishka was seated beside Zander, and he reached down to pet the top of the dog's head. Emil, from the other room, sensed the dog's allegiance was shifting and called to her. Reluctantly she went off down the hall. Zander followed for a few feet and then took a left toward the stairs. He carried his duffel over his shoulder, his backpack, and dirty clothes in his other hand as he climbed. Pictures lined the stairway. He knew them all. As a kid living with Emil, he had studied them, and now there was no need to look at faces from the past. On the landing to the left was Emil's bedroom with a private bath, and to the right were two guestrooms with a shared bathroom. Zander opened the door to his old room. Inside, everything was just as he had left it. The bed remained pushed up against the far wall with the window that faced the tree line at the back of the house. Another window on the right gave views toward town. The light hardwood floors gleamed in the sun. A trunk at the bottom of his bed contained toys he knew he'd left behind. The bookcase held childhood books—animals, plant identification, geography, and adventures of both fictional and non-fictional characters. Zander plunked down his duffel bag and backpack on the bed and the blue bedspread crumpled under the weight. He untied his boots and removed them. Then he unhooked the cord around the opening of the duffel bag and unlaced it, looking out the window to the back tree line. Finally, he pulled his last set of clean clothes from the duffel. He unbuttoned his jeans. Closing the door to the room, he grabbed the clean clothes off of the bed and headed to the shared bathroom. He flicked on the light, and the pale yellow of the bathroom walls shone brightly. Zander put his clean clothes on the stand next to the shower, pulled back the shower curtain, and turned on the water. Only then did he look in the mirror. He ran his hand along his chin; he needed a shave. He caught a glimpse of his knuckles in the reflection, and he held them out over the sink, looking at the healing cuts. He read his knuckles from left to right, the numerals 4-4-2 and 4-5-6. He gripped the edge of the white porcelain sink, leaned over, and hung his head. The steam began to roll around the bathroom, but Zander closed his eyes and saw Kit's face before him. He raised his head, looking at himself in the mirror that had begun to fog. Finally, he slid his pants and boxers to the floor, took off his socks and crumpled them, tossing them into the laundry bin. He stepped into the shower, pulling the curtain closed.

Downstairs, Emil closed the book with a snap when he heard the shower turn on. He patted Mishka a few times, rocking back and forth in his chair. Then he got up and straightened a few items on the end table. He moved the curtains out of the way and looked out to the mountain range. His lean frame rested against the window casing, his faded Levi's showing the even-more-faded spot on the back left pocket where his wallet rested. His soft flannel shirt was neatly tucked into his faded jeans, held up with a brown leather belt. The belt was hand tooled to show the animals from the Alaskan wilderness—bison, grizzly, a wolf, and an eagle in flight. He was smaller in stature than Zander, but the years of scouting, guiding, and hunting made him muscular and strong. His mind was swirling, the possible reasons why Zander had decided to return now. He looked at his own hands, weathered, worn, the skin showing age, and rubbed them together. He had noticed the healing cuts on Zander's hands, and then he thought of the stitches.

Upstairs, Zander turned off the water, pulled the shower curtain back, and grabbed a towel. He ran his hand back and forth through his hair, brushing off the water, then he trimmed his facial hair to a rough stubble. Drying off, he began to think about how to tell Emil about the trouble he was in. He dug out from his backpack the tube of cream and dabbed some along the line recently free of stitches. He went to toss it back in the bag and caught a glimpse of her sweater. He pulled it out for the first time since stashing it. He held it in his hands, staring at the threads. He looked around his room and, settling on a place to keep it, put it under his pillow. He pulled on his boots and laced them up. He slid on his vest and was buttoning the last four buttons on his shirt as he went down the stairs. Emil heard him and quickly sat down, pretending to read the book again just in time for Zander to enter the room.

"You got anything to drink?" he asked Emil.

"There's some stuff in the fridge," Emil replied.

Zander turned and headed back toward the kitchen. Emil closed the book again and followed after Zander.

"Alright, you've had your shower. Now tell me what is going on, Zander."

Zander pulled a soda out of the fridge, twisted the cap, and took a long drink. Emil stood watching him and Mishka joined them, lying down on the throw rug in front of the sink. Zander turned to face Emil but looked down at the floor.

"Zander?" Emil prompted in a whisper.

As Zander spoke, he looked into Emil's eyes. "I killed someone."

"Oh, Zander." Emil turned and ran his hand over his hair. "Who was it?"

"He was a kid I knew at the Academy."

"So, did he attack you?"

"No. He was attacking a person, a woman." Zander's voice caught on the word woman as he pictured Waverly. "In her house and I was there."

"So, you were defending her. But to kill him? What happened?"

"I just kept punching him, Emil. I saw her on the floor, what he had done to her, and I didn't stop," Zander stated.

"Zander, look at you. Even as a young boy you had this incredible strength, both mental and physical. What happened to your lessons here, your name—Reins, the ones you needed to harness your strength, the name I gave you?" Emil asked, his arms raised.

"Emil, I know. I messed up. In that moment, there was nothing else but—but . . . ," Zander looked out the window over the sink.

Emil asked, "But?"

"But her," Zander snapped.

"The girl on the floor?" Emil asked incredulously.

"Yes," Zander said in a whisper.

"Who is she?"

"She was someone I met, once," Zander said, looking again out the window.

"*Was?* Did she die too?" Emil asked.

"No," Zander turned his gaze back to the floor.

"Oh Zander, I'm sorry," Emil said.

"Anyway, I made my way back here. But now I'm not sure this is the best place for me," Zander said, looking at the front door.

"Zander, there is no better place for you. Here you have family, your friends, and we will protect you as best as we can. Here you can disappear into the wilderness and be gone, no questions asked," Emil said in an attempt to reassure Zander.

"I'm familiar with the disappearance into the wilderness and no questions being asked," Zander replied, referring to his father's death. Emil looked at Zander with compassion, but Zander turned away.

"There's one more thing," Zander said flatly. "The guy I killed, he was an addict, and he's the son of a powerful man." Now Zander looked seriously at Emil.

"How powerful?"

"His reach, if he wanted, could get up here."

"What's the name?"

"Mayfield."

Zander put the soda on the countertop and looked out the window again. Emil stood still, running the name Mayfield through his mind. It sounded familiar, but he couldn't place it.

"I can't live my life looking over my shoulder, Emil. I could hardly do it these past weeks," Zander said.

"Are you considering turning yourself in? You could take a plane back and explain what happened," Emil suggested.

"I'd die well before I saw the holding cell."

"Then there's only one thing to do. You take the documents; you take the job on the pipe. The previous pipe boy had the eight-four, you take that shift. You learn quick, take the eight-four leg, and spend most of your time out there." Emil pointed out the window to the woods, and beyond it to the pipeline. "If you're out there, most will forget you are even here. Leave your things here. The four months you're working in town, you can stay here, away from town," Emil planned.

Zander turned away from the sink and headed for the door.

"Where are you going?" Emil asked. He saw the gusts of wind pick up the dry earth from the drive.

"I need time to think," Zander responded. "Come on Mishka." The dog gladly got up from the rug and followed Zander out the door and down the stairs. Zander shoved his hands in the pockets of his vest and walked to the row of pines. Emil watched from the doorway, and, for a moment, he saw a young boy walking away from him.

Rupert finished with his pipe, went back into the house. He headed for the kitchen to fix himself a snack when the phone in the gate call box rang.

"Hello?"

"Mr. Thayer, this is Benny, you have a visitor here, a Miss Waverly Germaine. She says she knows you. Shall I let her up?"

"Yes, of course, send her up. Oh, and Benny, a phone call in advance would be appreciated before you send *any* guests up."

"Um, yes sir," Benny responded regretting that he had listened to both Mr. Mayfield and Chief Hayden to not inform Mr. Thayer of their arrivals earlier that morning.

Rupert placed the phone back in its cradle, grabbed a few grapes from the kitchen table and while popping them in his mouth went to the front door to greet his best friend's daughter, Waverly Germaine.

As Waverly exited her car, Rupert thought how much this young woman, whom he had seen grow-up before his eyes, resembled her parents.

"Hi, Mr. Thayer. I hope I'm not disturbing you," Waverly said as she got out of her car and went up the steps.

"Oh, it's never a bother to have a young beautiful woman call on me," he replied.

He kissed her cheek; and embraced her.

"It's been too long, Mr. Thayer, you really should come over. I'll fix you dinner," Waverly said.

"Ah, yes, let the rumors begin." He chuckled and welcomed her into his home.

For a moment Waverly stood before the dark wood stairs. Its curving banister had a gleam to it as if it had just been polished. The photographs that hung on the stairwell wall were of Natalie and Rupert's family, including some of the Germain's. An oil painting in an elaborate gold frame hung at the top of the stairs, a stern-looking man wearing a uniform was looking off in the distance.

Rupert ushered Waverly into the living room where a window seat made up the first level of the turret. The room boasted old furniture, dark floors, and built-in bookcases.

Rupert continued, "I went to the hospital to see you, but you were resting. I didn't want to bother you."

"I got the flowers. They were beautiful," Waverly replied.

"So is the whole matter..." He moved his hands from side to side, indicating finished.

"Well, not quite. My memories are coming back. Chief Hayden didn't say I was a suspect. Mr. Mayfield is upset with me. He thinks I'm being uncooperative with the investigation," she said.

"And are you?" Rupert motioned for her to sit on the blue velvet-upholstered curved-back sofa and waited for her to oblige before taking a seat in an old leather chair.

"I wouldn't say uncooperative, just hesitant to say too much, too soon, to the wrong people," she replied.

"Ah. When I heard Kit was missing, I thought 'Good riddance,'" he said in a firm tone.

Waverly looked at him with a bit of surprise.

"Don't get me wrong, I didn't want him to turn up dead. I just hoped he'd go somewhere else. Somewhere with more of what he liked to do with his life," he explained.

"I believe that before he died, he was hiding on the Mayfield Estate," she said.

"Of course he was. He was always the devil in plain sight," he stated.

"I'm not sure I understand," Waverly said.

"Well, you didn't grow up with him. Your father did well by you, sending you away to school as he did. Getting you away from this small town as a young girl with Kit in it," he stated.

"From what I've heard over the years, he didn't do anything too horrible."

"That pompous crook Mayfield would be happy to hear you say that. Since Kit was at the Academy and under my charge, as it were, I knew of all the things he did. All the times the police were involved. All the crying parents of boys who were missing teeth and had bloody noses and the girls he violated. There used to be a saying that people had here, 'If you needed a bit of extra money, get tangled up with Kit and then go see his father.' I think during Kit's childhood and adolescence more money passed through Harold Mayfield's hands to others in this town than through the bank. Kit terrorized all ages and all manner of God's creatures. Once I raised the rod to him, after I caught him with a teacher's watch engraved with the teacher's initials. Natalie's cat was found dead that night, hanging from the back porch of the main house," he stated.

"That's terrible! And you're certain it was him?" she asked.

"I knew it was him, but to prove it, like with so many of the monstrosities he committed, others took the blame or were paid off. He'd never stray from the estate, he can't," Rupert stated.

"Well, it's hard to leave a home, place, town that you hold dear. My father sent me away to school, but I came back," she said.

"You came back for all the right reasons, Waverly. This town thinks the world of you and your family. We all feel their absence." His voice broke a bit.

Rupert paused, finally he continued, shaking his head, "No, what I'm talking about is that Kit couldn't leave. His father's influence is here, his money is here. Within the four lines of this state, Kit could do no wrong. But if he were to go outside the lines his father's family has drawn, well, he'd be nothing."

"What does Mrs. Mayfield think of this? What was her part when Kit was growing up?" Waverly asked.

"Dripping in diamonds, pearls, and cashmere with her riding horses and her birthing contract fulfilled—"

"Her what?" she cut in.

"It was written into the marriage ceremony, no kidding, the marriage ceremony, that Kathleen Sarah Jewett now Mayfield, would be removed from the marriage if she did not, within eighteen months of their marriage, give birth to a son," Rupert stated.

"How 1700 of Mayfield!" Waverly exclaimed.

"1700 is right. Even further back than their fortune, no matter how crooked the line, can be traced," he said.

"Well, she had Kit, so she fulfilled her end," she said.

"And that's it, the end. Since the birth of Kit, she and Mayfield are hardly seen together, except for show. She never came to the Academy to be with Kit. Never saw her hold him as a baby or hold his hand as a boy," he explained.

"Mr. Thayer, what do you remember about Kit's friends? Anyone in particular he was close with?" she asked.

"When there was still a bit of good in Kit, there was one, Brad Jameson. Quiet boy. Smart boy. He was here on scholarship. He was close with Kit. Not for long, though, before he got caught up on Kit's path. Got blamed for a lot of what Kit did, but the difference was Brad's family couldn't pay for the damages. Brad kept silent, and Kit needed that," he replied.

"What about a boy named Zander? He was a bit older than Brad and Kit," she asked.

"Had lots of boys …" Rupert looked toward the mantle over the fireplace where graduating photos of his boys from the Gyrfalcon Academy stood.

Waverly cut in, "He had tattoos at a young age."

"Hard to forget that." He looked right at her.

"You don't forget much," she responded, holding his gaze.

"There was one time I remember. Kit turned on Brad and Zander was there. One of the teachers reported that Kit went to strike Brad with a chair over a game of chess, and Zander stepped in and got hit. The chair was in pieces, and Kit picked up a leg and hit Zander over and over, yelling all kinds of obscenities. The teacher didn't dare step in. Zander almost lost an eye during that incident."

"He never fought back?" she asked.

"He was a different kind, that one. A boy in a man's body at fifteen. He was taller than half our teachers, walked with a kind of what you kids call a swagger," Waverly laughed a bit when Rupert used the slang, it sounded so odd with his soft voice. He continued, "He was strong, so strong that the cook often asked him to open cans or lids when she couldn't. He was rough around the edges, and with all those tattoos, he made a hard impression. Not once did he strike Kit. Not once did he strike any of the boys."

"If he were older, why was he in the class with Kit and Brad?" she asked.

"We had no school records of him when he arrived at the Academy. He was assessed to be in that grade level, so that's where he went. He just showed up on the doorstep, as it were. He had a suitcase with all of his belongings in it and he held an envelope in his hands. His suitcase tag had his Christian name on it, Zander Blake, but when he signed for his allotted uniforms, he signed it 'Reins.' I remember because I asked him about that name. He just crossed it out and signed it Blake."

"He was scholarship as well?" she asked.

"You know, Waverly, you're not the first one to ask about Zander Blake today. You're not even the second. Mayfield was here this morning asking about him, and then that useless Chief Hayden came by after, asking for Zander's records."

He looked at her, she was trying not to give anything away with her face, but Rupert was so good at reading tells. He continued, "Even though it wasn't that long ago, the records we kept were handwritten or typed on an old-fashioned typewriter. Now everything's changing to those computers and floppy discs. The Academy is upgrading, and all of the old records are in the process of being added into the new system. My memory this morning wasn't as clear as it is now this afternoon."

He got up from his leather chair and went over to his desk. A fine, impressive desk, fit for a captain with carved feet in the shape of lion's paws. Rupert pulled a key from his pocket, unlocked a drawer, and pulled out a brown file folder that he put in Waverly's lap. While standing over her he said, "I told them both to check up in the admissions office. So many boxes have been moved over there from the old record house. And over the years, things have been moved from one place to another. Zander's file was probably misplaced or destroyed."

The folder now lay on her lap with a black and white photo clipped to the top. Even without the scar yet on his left eye, staring up at her from that little square, Rupert saw reflected in Waverly's eyes - recognition.

Zander and Mishka crossed through the pines. The cool air surrounded them. Emil was right. This was the only way. But still Zander tried to think of another, a way that involved him returning to Easton, to her. He leaned against a tree, looking out across the cleared space, beyond which were more pines. Mishka sat down at Zander's feet. Before them was the pipeline, and to his left was a wooden sign with a mile marker. High above them, soared a Gyrfalcon.

He folded his arms across his chest, his mind focused on the breeze as it picked up and moved the pines, but then his mind drifted back to her, standing in her kitchen, wearing her camisole, the feel of him behind her, the feel of her hands in his when he washed his hands with hers.

He tightened his arms around him, feeling a pinch where his wound was still raw. He would use the pain to make him focus and forget her. His eyes rested on the sedge blowing in the wind; the gusts had picked up. He trained his eye on the tops of the sedge and watched it ripple.

He imagined his hand along the back of her neck as he leaned into her. The light brush of her lips on his quickly slipped into him pushing his firmly against hers, which she returned.

He shook his head and tightened his arms. The pain from the still-sore wound sent a spike up his side. He heard a crumple of paper coming from inside his vest. The envelope Emil had given him with his new papers was tucked inside. He slid it out and pulled out the papers. Inside was a license, Social Security card, birth certificate, and the job offer of pipe boy with a designated route in this borough. Zander looked up at the pipe again and then down at Mishka who wagged her tail. Zander scratched the dog behind her ears.

"There it is," he said, looking back up to the pipe then down at the documents in his other hand. "That's all there is." He looked back down at Mishka. "Let's go home." He ruffled the dog's ears and pushed off the tree, heading back to Emil's house.

Silence. Emil had sat through an evening of silence. After Zander and Mishka returned from the outside, nothing was said between the two men. Each of them took their respective seats in the living room as if Zander was back in the ring and Emil his opponent. Mishka, not sure what was going on but sensing the tension and hearing each howl of the wind outside, lay between the men on the rug in the middle of the living room. Emil pretended to not care that Zander wasn't talking to him and read his book, although he couldn't remember what he had read. Zander wanted to say so much, but not knowing where to start, he stared at the fire in the fireplace. To Zander, everything was so familiar but different. Finally, without either saying a word, they separately went up the stairs and to their bedrooms. The click of their bedroom doors was the only sound in the house and Mishka, left alone, padded out to the kitchen, and laid on the rug listening to a silent house but raging nature outside.

By the next morning, Emil had had enough. "Come on," he said.

"Where are we going?" Zander asked.

"For a ride."

Emil and Zander climbed into Emil's silver truck and headed off down his gravel drive. Instead of taking the left toward town, Emil took a right. Zander had a sinking feeling when he saw the familiar fence, rundown now but still recognizable, and he turned to Emil, shifting in his seat. "Come on, man, I don't need to go up there."

"Yes, you do. You need to face this. I think it's a part of why it happened," Emil replied.

"No, it wasn't."

"Then you need to see what is yours. All of this is still yours," Emil said, glancing from side to side of the road ahead.

"I don't want it," Zander said, looking out the truck window at the long, aspen-lined long drive that cut through to pines and a clearing that had grown up, but Zander knew where to look.

Emil stopped the truck and turned off the engine. Silently they got out. Zander's eyes rested on the bits of fieldstone that could still be seen amongst the tall grass. It was the last place he had actually felt at home. All that was left after that night, the fire, was stones. Zander walked with one hand in his pocket. He let the tall grass flow through the fingertips of the other. He looked at the mile marker, a trail on either side of the pipe. It read 456. He looked to the trees on the opposite side of the pipeline. Emil, as if on cue, said, "Some fancy CEO from California bought the land over there. Had a vacation home built, and then the company went bankrupt, and the money dried up. It's for sale now. Other than that, not a soul around."

Zander kicked a few rocks around the foundation.

"This is all yours, Zander, whether you want it or not," Emil said.

"I never asked for it."

"You didn't have to. Your grandfather and your parents worked hard, and they enjoyed what they did. It is an accomplishment. One you should be proud of as well. It is a legacy they have left you," Emil said.

Zander turned to the north, looking up the pipeline. "But look at the cost."

"Something good can come out of this, Zander," Emil urged.

Zander turned his back on the pipeline and the foundation and headed back to the truck.

Zander awoke to the sound of men talking. He rolled over and looked at the alarm clock. He registered the time but had no idea of the day. He rolled over on his back and put an arm over his eyes. At last, he felt hunger. He swung his feet out of the bed and put them on the floor. His elbows rested on his knees, and he held his head in his hands. He could still hear the men talking from somewhere outside. He let his hands drop and turned his head to the side. He could make out Emil's voice and one other, which sounded familiar. He stood, stretching, then he straightened his boxers and pulled a t-shirt on and headed down the stairs. He made his way to the kitchen and ran some water in a glass. He moved to the kitchen door and slowly moved the curtain a bit to the side. He saw Quinn, an elder in the Athabaskans, with a younger man standing next to him. The younger man had long raven-black hair, caramel-colored skin, eyes that appeared black, and an impish grin on his face. The men shook Emil's hand and then got into a blue pickup truck. Zander glanced around and saw Emil looking at a black truck beside his silver one. Emil was heading back to the house, and Zander stepped away from the door and took one more drink from the glass. He opened the fridge door and took out some brown eggs, milk, and butter.

Emil came in through the door. "I see you're up."

"Hmmm," Zander responded.

"Slept two days," Emil said.

Zander paused, cracking an egg on the side of the pan that had been sitting on the stove burner. A pad of butter was floating in the base, heated by the gas fire below. He finished cracking the egg on the side of the pan.

"That was Quinn. You remember him?" asked Emil.

Zander nodded his head in response.

"Chip, the boy with him," Emil continued, "he's Dika and Patuk's son, the ones who run the General Store and Post Office. He also works the pipe. He just got himself a new truck. Didn't need his old one."

Zander took a spatula and broke the yokes of the eggs in the pan. He turned to Emil with a look of curiosity on his face.

"It's yours now. You'll need a set of wheels up here," Emil said as he tossed the keys to Zander, who caught them.

"Thanks, I'll pay you for the truck," Zander replied.

"Yes, you will, but not with money. You need to get back to working on yourself, Zander. You need to get a hold of your reins," Emil said sternly.

"Emil—," Zander began, but was cut off.

"There's a meeting tonight at Quinn's. We're going," Emil left the kitchen and went to the living room, expecting a fight, but Zander just used the spatula to move the eggs in the pan and grabbed a plate from the cupboard. He slid the eggs out of the pan onto the plate, poured himself a glass of milk, and sat down in one of the chairs in the breakfast nook to eat the first meal he'd had in a long time.

In the light of the fire, Zander heard words from a Native tongue pass over him. Smoke cleared his mind and flushed his skin. His eyes reflected the flames from the bonfire, and he felt the restless spirit inside himself along with another spirit, something lighter. The two were joined, but he could feel the lighter one take hold of him, and her face flashed before his eyes. He called to her, his hand moved to his bare chest, down to where a healing five-inch line bumped up under his skin. But then her image was gone, and he felt the pain of the restless spirit, one who had become uncontrollable, take hold. He felt the punches landing on him, the anger of the injustice of the deaths of his grandfather, father, and mother. He saw Kit's anger unleashed on her. As he swung his fists, Kit's face changed and reflected the demons, the faces of demons, ones he could not control any more than Zander could his own. Zander—dripping with sweat, breathing hard, chest heaving—stood and walked away from the fire, away from the men and into the night.

Zander bolted upright; something had woken him. It was still dark outside. He looked at the clock—1 a.m. He laid back, rubbing his hands over his face and stared at the ceiling, calming his breathing. He was drenched in sweat. A sleeve from her sweater stuck out from under his pillow. He touched it then laid back down, his face inches from the sleeve and breathed in her scent, which lingered in the material. He rolled onto his back. In a few hours he would go for a run to clear his head.

Today he was going to go into town and meet the crew of pipe boys, well, the ones working in the office at this time of the year. It was time for him to put the next part of Emil's plan in motion. Coming back from his run, he approached Emil's house and slowed. He watched the cool mist roll through the surrounding pines;

it gave an eerie atmosphere. He climbed the stairs and headed for a shower. Laid out on his bed were clothes and his documents to present at the office. Ready to start his day, he went down the stairs and was greeted with the warm smell of breakfast cooking. He grabbed two pieces of toast from the plate Emil had fixed for himself and, with a bite in his mouth said, "See you later," as he opened the door.

"You want some breakfast?" But Zander was gone. Still Emil called after him, "Gganaa'."

He removed two caribou sausage links from the frying pan and put them on the plate, where he could've sworn he had left two pieces of buttered toast.

Zander drove into town, gliding along the straight and wide. He saw the pipe company's new building and the trucks parked outside with the familiar logo on them. He remembered sitting at their kitchen table with his father, designing that logo. He pulled into a spot out front and looked down the side road where the old trailer was, a few double-wides partitioned together to make the offices. He remembered climbing up the metal stairs and the freezing cold metal railing he had once touched with his bare hand. He flexed his left hand, remembering the sting of the cold. The smell of tobacco would linger in those offices with the heavy smell of toner from the copiers, always buzzing with the lights flashes from under their lids. He was brought back to the present when the glass door to the building opened and the young man who had been with Quinn outside Emil's house stepped outside. A glove dangled from

Chip's mouth. He noticed Zander and walked over to the driver's side of the truck and Zander rolled down the window.

"Hey, man, good to see you. I'm Chip. How's she treating you?" Chip asked after taking the glove out of his mouth, looking at the truck from side to side.

"Good. Thanks for selling her, I'm Zander."

"Well, I know how attached Emil is to that silver can of his. That has got to be ancient, I mean he had that thing when I was young," Chip said with a laugh.

"He had it when I was young," Zander said with a smile, looking at the glass doors leading into the building.

Chip made a whistle between pursed lips and raised his eyebrows. There were ten years between the two men, but since Zander had been gone for all of Chip's life, it seemed more like twenty. Chip reminded Zander of Brad, with the effortless and comfortable way about him.

"Will's waiting on you, man. I'd say good luck but, you don't need it. I'll see you later," Chip said.

Zander got out of his truck. "See you," Zander responded. The building before him was a tall, sweeping glass structure, the curve of the walls jutting out from the straight and wide. The architect had designed it to reflect the form of an iceberg. Zander walked to the glass doors, noticing a scanner for a badge or ID, but having neither he approached the doors slowly. They opened once the secretary noticed Zander outside and pressed the button to let him in. The glass walls allowed those inside to see all the happenings on the straight and wide, as well as down the cross street. The lobby floor was made from grey slate. The ceiling rose up to a point, giving a great view of the sky. The lobby was a single large area with a desk for the secretary, and a corridor led to an exit. From where Zander stood, he could see the outer buildings, the company logo on their sides. At the farthest end of the lobby was a doorway. Zander nodded at the woman who reminded him of some of the women who visited their grandsons at the Academy. She was holding out her hand. "You must be the rookie. I'm Millie, just the secretary."

As Zander shook her hand, a man with red hair and pale green eyes approached them.

"Hey there, right on schedule. You must be Zander, I'm Will Parkst. I'm the senior pipe boy here. And don't let her fool you. Millie is the heart of this place."

Millie sat back down and flapped her hand at Will as if shooing away a fly.

Zander held out his hand and shook Will's. Will noticed the silence, along with the strength of Zander's handshake. He wasn't exactly what Will had imagined when he took the phone call from Stuart informing him that Zander would be the new hire. To fill the silence, Will continued, "Well, come this way. I've got a space cleaned in the office and all the paperwork is gathered for you. Let's first get you a badge so that you'll have access right away."

The two walked through the large lobby toward the doorway that led to the large office where the pipe boys all had their desks. The desks lined the office walls, all facing the center. A whiteboard held a list of names with what looked like miles beside them hung on one wall. On another wall were a dart board and a bulletin board full of notices. Off of this office were other doorways leading to a large supply closet, a break room, a small workout room, a restroom, and one marked as an exit.

Will took a seat at a desk with a computer on it and motioned for Zander to sit in the chair next to the desk. Zander took the seat and looked around the room. Enlarged photos graced the walls, a photographic timeline of the pipeline's history. Aerial views of the land that was to be surveyed for the pipe, the first shovel to break ground, the people who were involved. From his childhood, Zander recognized a few of the faces staring back at him. His eyes rested on his grandfather's face. Distracted, he didn't hear Will's first question. Will lifted his head from the paperwork before him and followed Zander's eyes, which were looking at a photo on the wall of a man in his fifties smiling at the camera. He stood next to a theodolite.

"Pretty neat, huh? I found these photos in one of the last desks I cleaned out in the old office building. The company thought it would be a good idea to have them enlarged and displayed, like a memorial of sorts."

Zander turned his head toward Will and looked at the paperwork on the desk. Will, realizing Zander wasn't going to comment, turned back to the paperwork. Millie came in with a man pulling a dolly loaded with reams of paper.

"Okay, so the first form is pretty basic. I need your name, date of birth, address, and identification."

Zander fished out his wallet and pulled out his new license. "Zander Blake," he said as he handed the license to Will.

"This one says Reins on it," Will questioned, reading the license.

Zander looked to the storage area where Millie's trained ear was listening in on their conversation and the deliveryman was taking his time unloading the boxes. Zander mumbled, "Reins, Zander Reins."

Will tried not to show his hesitation. He remembered the phone call from Stuart, third in line to the CEO of the company. "Good morning, Lower Borough office, Will Parkst speaking," Will said as he picked up the phone.

"Will, it's Stuart Hughes. How are things going up there?" he asked.

"Good. We're all making the rounds. The town is good, morale is good. Any news on Craig Dawson's replacement?" Will asked.

"About that. This is coming from above; I mean from the man himself. You're going to get a rookie soon. Zander is his name; he should be there before the first snow. You'll need to show him the ropes and get him settled in."

"Any prior experience?" Will asked.

"No idea, just make it happen. And Will," Stuart said, pausing for Will to respond.

"Yeah?"

"The way this whole thing is being handled, don't ask questions. Understood?" Stuart cautioned.

"Yes, sir."

"Take care."

"You too, sir." Will hung up the phone and sat back in his chair. He remembered when he was applying for this position and all the hoops he had to jump through and the scrutiny that he was under for all the security clearances, and here was this unknown. Well, thought Will, he must be known to the right person to get the position just like that. Will couldn't help but wonder if this rookie was being placed with them because of the abruptness way Craig had left. Maybe the company was suspicious. As far as employment went, this job was good, decent benefits, good pay, and room for advancement. Will himself had gone from low man on the totem pole to lead in a few years' time.

Will noted the discrepancy in Zander's last name, but as instructed, he didn't question it. Millie and the deliveryman walked from the supply closet out to the main lobby.

"Well, one form done. Let's head over, get your photo taken, and get your ID done."

The men walked back out into the lobby area, heading for the exit to the outbuildings. Before the exit was a small alcove where a tripod and camera were set up. Zander stood against the wall in front of the camera.

"When you're ready," Will said, standing behind the camera.

"Hmmm," Zander mumbled, keeping his hands in his pockets, and looking right at the lens. Will took that as an affirmative and clicked the shutter button. A few minutes later, Zander's badge was being printed from the machine, put on a lanyard, and handed to Zander, who slipped it over his head.

Will rattled off, "A few nondisclosure forms to sign and last the personal form, and I'll need an address for your check. I should have just grabbed it from your license."

"You can just hold them here," Zander mumbled, knowing Emil's address was on his license.

"Okay, we can do that. The notices, bulletins, you can get here. They'll be posted," Will stated. He had an itch to ask a question but bit his tongue. His suspicions were raised.

"Let's head out to the range. How good are you with guns?" asked Will.

"Fine," Zander replied.

"It's required that we carry both a pistol and a rifle and we need to be qualified each time we're off the pipe, so regularly once a year with the office time. So, let's go see your marks," Will said. He'd often heard people who claimed to be fine with guns, but then found out they either weren't comfortable with them or couldn't pass the qualifying requirement.

It had been a long time since Zander had fired a gun. He had been raised around guns and knew how to use them, clean them, and respect them. Both his grandfather and father had taken Zander into the woods to practice shooting, to track and hunt. After the first round left the chamber, it all came back to Zander, all the words from his grandfather and father about the stance, the breathing, the slight pull of the trigger. He passed with flying colors, and Will sensed this guy was someone to be reckoned with. The rest of Zander's orientation involved a tour of the stables with the mounts and the hanger.

"How comfortable are you with horses?" asked Will.

"Good," Zander replied as he headed over to one mount and moved his hands along the flank and then up the nose and forehead. Will guessed that Zander was probably more comfortable around horses than with people.

"Last stop is the hanger," Will said, as he gave a few pats on the head to a rust-brown horse that showed obvious interest in Will. Zander and Will walked through the stable to the other end. Will slid the door open, then Zander pulled it closed behind them and followed Will to a larger building in the back.

"In the hanger we have four-wheelers, trucks, and snow machines. You will have one of each assigned to you. And the chopper. You have your flying license?" Will asked.

"No."

"Three of us do, wouldn't hurt for you to get it. We assist with search and rescue and sometimes the conservationists need our help tracking animals," Will said.

Zander nodded.

"You familiar with the town?" Will realized he had been doing nothing but asking Zander questions, the exact thing Stuart had advised him not to do. He opened his mouth to say never mind, but Zander answered the question before he could.

"I know it. I know the land that surrounds it, the borough."

"While we're in town, we are expected to help out the local law enforcement, most of the time we are the local law enforcement. We do traffic control when there are festivals, we look into any kind of disturbance reported, mostly we keep the peace. You good with all of that?" Will asked as they reached the lobby area again.

"Hmmm," Zander said, nodding his head and looking at the mountains in the distance.

And with that, Zander's first day of orientation was at an end.

"Tomorrow, then, 6 a.m. sharp, you and I will go out on a leg. Get you exposed to the duties you can expect to manage while being one of us," Will said.

"Sounds good," Zander said.

Will held out his hand, and Zander shook it.

"Welcome to the pipe," Will said, smiling. Zander headed for the door. He scanned his ID at the screen, a green light lit up above the door, and he pushed through to the parking lot. It was dusk. He got into his truck, turned the engine over, and headed back up the mountain to Emil's house. He watched the mountain range before him turn from a jagged outline to darkness against the sky.

Chip returned to the office a few minutes after Zander had left. Millie was at her desk, inputting Zander's information into the system.

"Hiya, Millie," Chip said as he strolled into the building.

"Hey, Chip. Where have you been?" Millie asked, her fingers moving quickly across the keyboard.

"I went to say hello to Tiffany," Chip said with that same impish grin Zander had seen on his face.

"Oh, it's Tiffany this week, is it?" Millie asked as she stopped typing and eyed Chip over her glasses, teasing him.

Chip gave a short laugh. "So, we're back to a full house around here," he replied. "Anyone still around?" he asked.

"Will's in the back and Welch should be here shortly for the night," Millie stated, turning back to the papers on her desk.

"Cool, have a good night." Chip headed to the back office. There he saw Will flipping through some files in an old filing cabinet they had brought over from the old building.

"Hey, Will!" Chip called as he headed to the break room.

Will turned, startled. "Oh, hey Chip. How's the night looking?"

Chip came back out with a pear that he was biting into. With a piece of the fruit in his mouth he responded, "Quiet, just like the day. What are you looking for? I didn't know there was stuff in that filing cabinet."

Chip walked through the room again, placing the pear on his desk, and then went into the bathroom. Will replied, "Nothing. There's just old paperwork. You never know when you might need to recall something from twenty years ago." He turned to the empty room, then turned back to the drawer while his fingers found the file he was looking for and pulled it out. The label on the file read *Blake*. Inside were maps of property, blueprints for two houses, and a perpetual deed signed by Geoffrey, Jacob, and Klara Blake, along with Charlie Jewett. Chip sauntered out of the bathroom, grabbed the pear off his desk, and bit into it again.

"So, you found what you were looking for?" Chip reached to the side of his desk where there were labeled hooks for keys. He put his truck keys on one and lifted off a set labeled four-wheeler. Will put the file in a drawer of his desk, then turned to face the whiteboard. He picked up a marker and wrote Zander's name under his where Craig's use to be.

"Oh, it's nothing. New guy started today. I'm going to take him out with me tomorrow, show him a leg on the pipe, just so he can get a taste of it."

While Will spoke, Chip remembered his flashlight was dead and went into the supply closet to get fresh batteries. He flipped open the top of a box and grabbed a few to have some spares and put them in his pockets. He took a quick look around to see if he needed anything else, but decided his ride was well packed. Will finished writing Zander's name, then stepped back and looked at the board. All assigned lines were filled. He turned around, and the room was empty again. Will flashed an annoyed look. *That kid could ghost out of a room like vapor.* He grabbed his coat off the back of his chair and pulled it on one arm and then the other. Chip came out of the storage room and Will watched him re-materialize. "You ever stay in one place for longer than three seconds?" Will teased.

"Naw man, gotta keep it moving and shaking!" Chip exclaimed. "He'll catch on quick, no doubt," Chip said of Zander.

"I think so," Will agreed. He was heading for the restroom. "He's not a talker."

"You can say that again," Chip said.

Will stopped suddenly. "You know him?"

Chip slowed down, realizing he had made a mistake. When he and Quinn went to Emil's that day to drop off Chip's truck, Quinn took Chip aside and told him it was time for Chip to be taken seriously within the borough. He was the son of Patuk and Dika, respected people; he was working on the pipe and protecting the interests of the people, the land, and the animals. Quinn told him that Emil had a man living with him, that this man had returned and was part of the land and the people as well, and that Chip should honor him by not talking to outsiders about the man.

Chip backtracked and cleared his throat. "I do now. Ran into him as I was leaving earlier." Will's face showed that he was not convinced. Chip, knowing Will would ask more questions, launched the pear into the waste bin. "Well, I'm outta here. Have a good night Will," and then, poof, Chip was gone.

Will heard Chip say goodnight to Millie, he turned on the lamp on his desk and took the file out of the drawer. He opened the cover of the file and took a closer look at its contents. The paper had yellowed, and the grey ink had faded even lighter. But the deed was easy to read: *On this day, the Universal Supply Companies and Holdings does set into perpetual term for the family and descendants of Geoffrey Blake from milepost marker 442 – 456 in the amount of six hundred acreage west of the pipeline.* "Zander Blake . . . Zander Reins? Who are you?" asked Will of no one, but as he looked up, he wouldn't have been surprised if Chip had reappeared.

Zander pulled into Emil's drive, his headlights illuminating the house. He saw Mishka on the steps, and
once he got closer the dog bounded down the steps, tail
wagging. Zander killed the lights and the engine of the
truck and parked, greeted by the happy dog as he exited.
Emil swung open the front door. "How'd you make out?"

"Fine," Zander replied, paying more attention to
Mishka at his side.

"Will's a nice man, respected, was in the military
for a while," Emil continued.

"Hmmm," Zander mumbled as he walked past Emil
and into the kitchen.

"Thought you might be hungry. Made some stew,"
Emil offered.

"Sounds good." Zander sat down at the table where Emil had set two places, fresh bread was sliced, and butter waited to be spread. Emil bent down to give a bowl of food to Mishka, and then brought the pot over from the stove with a spoon. Zander helped himself out of the pot and waited for Emil to serve himself and sit down.

"You gonna say anything other than 'fine' about the day?" Emil said as he took his seat.

Zander shook his head no.

"You want to tell me anything else about your life? What it was that you were doing?" Emil pressed.

Zander went to shake his head again but thought better of it. As he looked at Emil over the shared meal, he offered, "I was a boxer."

"Oh, is that right? Well, by the size and look of you I'm sure you did alright for yourself."

Zander said nothing. The only noise was the clink of his spoon hitting the bowl. Emil pressed, "Did you?"

"I held my own."

"Ahh," Emil said. Zander looked up at him, a questioning look on his face.

"'Ahh' what?" Zander asked.

"Nothing," Emil said, quickly dismissing the thought, as it was linked to why Zander came back. Emil surmised that Zander would be looked at differently in the eyes of the law due to his fighting background. "And you made a living from that?" Emil asked, hoping to shift Zander's attention.

"I drove for a company," Zander added. He was using a piece of bread to mop up the rest of the stew in the bowl.

"You didn't settle down, or have someone?" Emil asked.

This question went too far. Zander pushed away from the table and went over to the sink. He washed his dishes, putting them in the drainer, and then turned to the stairs. "Thanks for supper."

And then he was gone up the stairs to his room. He hung the lanyard on the bedpost, then took off his vest and flung it over the back of the chair. He unlaced his boots and kicked them off. He sat on the edge of the bed for a moment, then turned quickly and removed her sweater from its hiding place. He held it between his hands and hung his head. Clenching it between his fists, he laid down on his bed looking out the window. He watched the night sky begin to glint. He knew she'd never get over what had happened that night and probably would never forgive him or want anything to do with him. All the trouble surrounding him, but he couldn't help wanting her. He couldn't help letting his mind, just for the moment, imagine a situation that would never happen.

Emil was left downstairs cleaning up the rest of the table. He poured the remaining stew into Mishka's bowl and patted her on the head, saying, "Well, as more unfolds it makes more sense." He began scrubbing the stew pot, looking out the window. A shooting star fluttered across the sky and left a thin, sparkling veil behind. "He's pushing hard, isn't he?" Emil asked, and Mishka lifted her head and cocked it to the side. Emil watched the stardust left behind twinkle and fade. "I don't know if the push is toward her or away from her. I'm worried that, if he doesn't either close that door or open it fully, with him just standing there, half in and half out, it will close forever on its own."

When Zander pulled up to work the next morning, fifteen minutes early, there was one other truck in the lot. He got out of the truck, pulled his ID from the lanyard around his neck, and held it up to the screen on the metal post. The light turned green and hearing the click of the lock releasing, he went in. The building had soft lights on, illuminating the hall. In the doorway to the office, he ran his hand along the wall and clicked on the light. He looked for a moment at the photo of his grandfather. He saw a desk on the opposite side of the room from Will's. It was empty of anything personal. He saw Chip's desk, recognizing it by the name plaque on it. On a desk labeled Welch sat a cup with coffee sitting cold on it. The desks of the other two pipe boys, who he had yet to meet and might never, given the structure of their work, had various desk accessories on them. Over the backs of their chairs hung flannel shirts, flags marking their territory. He guessed the empty one was to be his. He studied the whiteboard with the names of the pipe boys on it with their schedules and assignments with countdowns of arrivals. It was blank next to Zander's name. Written next to Will's was twelve months UFN (Until Further Notice). On Will's desk, Zander saw a wedding picture of Will with a woman. He was wearing a uniform, and they looked at one another with great affection. Then Zander saw the old file. It was under a pile of papers, but Zander picked out his name, Blake. Before he could look at it, Will came through the door.

"You're here early."

"Thought I'd get my bearings of the office," Zander said.

"Well, that desk is yours right there," Will said pointing to the empty desk opposite his. "Welch should be around here somewhere," he said looking around, then, not seeing or hearing anyone, he continued, "Supplies are in the closet. You want to set that up now?"

"No, let's get out there," Zander said, glancing again at the file on Will's desk.

"Four-wheelers are all fueled up," Will said as he slid the file into a drawer. "So, I told Millie you'll be needing company gear. Just give her your sizes and she'll get you outfitted. You can do that tomorrow," Will said as they walked together out the back door to the hanger.

"Okay."

"Without a uniform, you will find that not many will respond to you," Will said.

Zander climbed onto his four-wheeler and started it up. Will called over his shoulder, "We'll just head up behind the building and go up the mountain a ways. I'll show you what we look for, how we log our miles, and how we check in." Zander nodded and followed Will's lead. They rode along the buildings where a path had been worn into the ground for the pipe boys' trucks, four-wheelers and snow machines. They continued on and hit the dirt trail that ran the length of the pipe. Will stopped at the first mile marker out of town and let the quad idle for a bit. Zander pulled up beside him.

"When we're out on the pipe we check for defacing, damage, signs of terrorism, anything that isn't already logged. You will need to get familiar with your part of the pipe, know it inside and out. We also watch for any new migration patterns, any new tracks. The land on either side of the pipe is either owned or for sale. Some is part of the conservation. So, we need to respect whichever it is. We log it all here in the books." Will pulled a clipboard of log sheets from the side pack of his four-wheeler. "When they're full, we put them in our logbooks in the office." Then Will pointed to the map, "Here's a guard shack. We use them in inclement weather. They aren't much, but they'll shield you from the weather and there are stoves in them for cooking and heat. Any damage to the shacks, any sign of tampering, you make note of it. When reported on the check-in, the company will decide if it's worth investigating.

Let's ride to that one, and I'll show you what they look like inside."

After riding for a few more mile markers, they pulled up next to a one-room shack built of wood with a shingled roof. Windows with locked blinds on them were on three sides, and the door was solid wood. Nailed to it was a no-trespassing sign with a clear keep-out sign tacked below it. A large padlock held the door closed against any intruders.

"This is a skeleton key," Will said, as he pulled a key from a ring locked to his belt. "You can use it for any of the shacks. In the mild weather most of us camp out, but if you prefer a roof over your head, this is it."

Will pushed the door open, but it stuck a bit. Inside there was barely enough room for the two of them to stand. The stove sat in a corner. On the longer wall was the bed, and a small table with one chair and a cupboard above the table were along the opposite wall.

"Not many comforts, but we try to keep the cupboard stocked with provisions and there's a first aid kit."

Will opened the door to the cupboard, which revealed cans of various soups, condensed milk, bottled water, instant coffee, and a can of tea.

"To be on the safe side," Will said, turning to Zander as he closed the cupboard door, "I'd check the expiration dates. Also, make sure you have enough food in your packs before you leave town. These shacks get vandalized often and ransacked. Not so much the ones closest to town, but the ones further out. Again, we make note, the company decides whether to investigate or not or to rebuild or not. Expect some issues further up the pipe."

Zander walked out of the shack and Will followed, then clicked the padlock in place.

"Let's head up the pipe and check in some more miles."

As the markers continued, Zander kept an eye on the pipe and watched Will, looking around and taking in everything. Zander knew where they were headed. Soon they'd be at where Zander's family's land began. He knew Will had read the file and probably remembered his slip with his last name. They passed the 442 mile marker and Will idled his quad again.

"All looks good. Did you notice anything?" Will tested Zander.

"There were some broken branches on the 398 that led off into the woods. Could've been an animal crashing through. On the way back we should see if there are any tracks or bits of fur on the broken branches," Zander replied.

"Good spotting," Will said. He cut his engine and rested his hands on his legs, looking up at the pipe's path and took in a deep breath. Zander killed his engine.

"Zander, your business is your business, but if we're going to be partners, we need to trust one another." Zander knew that the job was more than a job, they—meaning the pipe boys—were more than just co-workers. They needed more than trust, they were brothers, they would rely on one another, and a bond needed to be forged between them. Even with the ones who were thousands of miles away, they needed to know that they could count on the ones in town to take care of their loved ones left behind and vice versa.

"Ask what you need to," Zander said.

Will gestured his hand to the left. "You're mixed up in all of this, aren't you?" he asked, looking at Zander.

"Hmmm," Zander nodded looking at Will.

"So, you're somebody then."

Zander sighed, looking down at his hands, at the ink on his knuckles. "I am no one," he said, and looked up at Will.

Will considered this, slightly nodding his head. He finally gave a half shrug and said, "Let's head back. It'll be dark soon and my wife will be waiting."

They started up their quads and turned them back on the trail heading to town, stopping briefly at the 398 marker and looking at the broken branches. Cloven hooves led to the tree line and through the woods, most likely a lone caribou seeking a herd. Will marked it on the log sheet, tucked it back into the side pocket, and gave a nod to Zander. The two of them rode the rest of the way to town, not seeing anything but calm nature.

Will swiped his ID to open the hanger door. They rolled their four-wheelers into the large cover. Will turned to Zander. "That one is yours, the keys you keep on the side of your desk. You're responsible for telling whichever one of us is in the office that it needs maintenance; you will need to keep it fully stocked."

Zander nodded and then headed with Will into the main office. Zander slid the key ring onto the hook affixed to the side of his desk and watched Will do the same.

He logged in the miles and noted the broken branches with the caribou movement. Zander leaned on the desk, watching what Will did and the order.

"The man who was my partner just left, no notice. Just left. When I was told you'd be coming, I was pulled off the pipe to get you settled. The other boys," he said, looking at the whiteboard, "have been filling in. Mostly Chip, looking after the pipe assigned to me. Because our leg of the pipe is close to town, we can check in more often in the office. So, when you make a loop up there and come back, you can stop in town get some provisions you need, do some office work, and stay a night or two in your own bed, then head back out. Right now, we've got Chip's partner Milo out on the pipe with their section and Chip's in town. Marty and Welch are partners. Welch is in town and Marty is out on the pipe, and then there's you and me. I'll be doing a twelve straight starting next month until you feel ready to get out there."

As Will spoke, he pointed to the whiteboard in front of them where the pipe boy's names were listed. Next to their names were their shifts, either eight-four or four-eight for the months on the pipe or in the town. The pipe boys whose name had the eight-four next to it would be up on the pipe for eight months out of the year and then spend four months in the town working at the office and helping out the local law enforcement. When working in the office, they were responsible for the upkeep of the vehicles and the care of the mounts. The overnight shift was alternated between the pipe boys in the town. They would also carry a walkie-talkie at all times for when the pipe boys on the pipe radioed in, then write the mile marker next to their names. Zander looked beside his name, there was nothing assigned to him yet. He took the extra magnet for eight-four that had been beside Will's name and put it next to his name.

"Oh no man, until you can get settled—" Will said.

Zander turned to Will. "I'm settled."

Will sensed that Zander wasn't one to argue with, and he wasn't looking forward to being out on the pipe for twelve straight months away from Christine.

"Well, okay then. Here's a list of items we've put together over the years of things we all have found useful or needed while out there." Will handed a sheet of paper to Zander. "It's broken down into seasons. We're on the cusp of seasons, catching the end of fall and beginning of winter."

Zander looked at the list and nodded his head. He pushed off the desk, "I'll leave the day after tomorrow," Zander said, heading for the hallway.

"Zander, you sure? You'll be out there on your own for months at the beginning of the harshest season."

"I'm sure," Zander called from the lobby area as he flashed his ID at the screen inside the lobby. The light went green, and he pushed through the doors.

Before Emil could ask anything, Zander spoke. "I signed up for the eight-four." He looked at the table, set for the night's meal of caribou steak and potatoes.

"When do you leave?" asked Emil.

"Day after tomorrow."

"Doesn't give much time to get all that you'll need."

"The company will provide gear," Zander responded as he washed his hands. After drying them on the kitchen towel, he took a seat across from Emil.

"Gear is fine, but you need to be ready, in all ways, to be alone out there, to face yourself."

Zander looked at Emil and paused in cutting his steak.

"If you feel as if you are ready," Emil backtracked, "then we just need to get you ready with food and supplies. I can gather some things from around here," he said, trying to be helpful.

"I can do all of that," Zander said.

Emil slammed his fist down. "Damn it, Zander, you don't have to do everything on your own. You're not alone anymore."

"Maybe I want to be."

"If that were true, you wouldn't be wanting and willing like you have been."

Zander rose from the table, dumping his plate into Mishka's bowl, and washed his dishes, putting them in the dish drain, then headed for the stairs. Emil looked at Mishka, "Well, I have one more supper with him. Maybe we can make it through that." He rose and put his own scraps in Mishka's bowl, saying, "Don't get used to this," but he wasn't sure if he was saying that for Mishka's benefit or for his own.

Zander, up in his room, set to work pulling together things he had that he would need to take with him. He didn't have much. When he finished with that, he undressed and got into bed, looking out the window. He made a mental list of the things he would need from the General Store in town.

Downstairs in the kitchen Emil looked over the list Zander had left on the counter and began to pull items together, making a pile on the table. Opening and closing closet and cupboard doors, he gathered matches, flashlights, batteries, beef and caribou jerky, bottled water, oatmeal, and canned fruit. He also gathered warm gloves made from the best beaver and a good pair of snowshoes. Mishka watched Emil go from one room to the next, bringing items back and forth, mumbling all the while under his breath.

Zander went downstairs for his morning run and paused when he saw the kitchen table piled with the items Emil had gathered. He ran his hands over the snowshoes and the mittens, feeling their softness, and then headed out the door. The last remaining light of the aurora borealis was fading in green waves across the sky as Zander took off down the drive. Even with all the items Emil had gathered, there were still a few things Zander wanted. There was no other option. He'd have to go into town, into the General Store.

Emil was up when Zander came back to the house. He was making breakfast, starting his day. Not a word was exchanged. When Zander came downstairs after his shower, there were two places set at the table. The men looked at one another. "I thought we'd try breakfast again," Emil said. The gear and provisions were lined up on the counter and floor. Zander looked at the items again and considered them. "Not sure about you going into the General Store, the most social hub in the town," Emil said, as if reading Zander's mind.

Zander knew that by social hub Emil meant gossip wheel. Not that the news of Zander's arrival hadn't already hit the far corners of the borough, but why flaunt it when he should be keeping a low profile. Zander sat down at the table and began eating his eggs and his piece of bacon.

"While you're gone, is there anything you need me to do?"

Zander shrugged.

"I'll be going into town myself today, so it won't be an inconvenience. Do you want anything particular for your journey?"

Zander shook his head.

"It's as if you are not even here. I might as well be talking to Mishka!" Emil pointed to the dog, who perked up, expecting a treat. Emil stood at the sink, running water over a pan.

"I don't remember it being this hard when you were a boy," Emil said, exasperated.

Zander responded as he shut the front door, "You didn't talk as much." Emil turned abruptly, an annoyed look on his face, as the door closed. He looked at the table, and there was a list of items in Zander's handwriting for him. Emil looked at his plate. *I could've sworn I had two pieces of bacon left.*

"Well, you're a strapping one, aren't you?" Millie said as she eyed Zander over the rims of her glasses. Zander was removing his vest to get ready to try on some of the uniform jackets. He stood in the supply closet with her, where a large locker spanned the length of the back wall. It had two accordion-style doors that Millie pushed open, revealing, from left to right, seasonal clothing and gear. Spring breakup rain gear, consisting of jackets, pants, and hoodies; summer gear of lightweight cargo pants and polo shirts; fall lightweight jackets with button-down shirts; and Winter gear of snow pants, hats, goggles, gloves, long johns, thermal tops and bottoms, and all-terrain boots at the far right.

"Welch is taller, but broad like you in the shoulders, he takes a—" Millie was sifting through the hangers.

Zander offered, "If you have better things to do . . . ."

Millie turned, giving a look that Zander had seen before. It had been used on Chip earlier that morning. It conveyed, *hush or face the consequences.* Millie turned back to the clothing.

"Nonsense, Zander. This is important. I need to make sure my boys are ready to face the elements out there."

Zander did a side smile when Millie said, "my boys." He had seen how she interacted with Will, Chip, and Welch. She kept them in line, made sure they cleaned up after themselves, and did not hold back her opinion— even when not asked—about anything and everything. Millie also gave words of wisdom and encouragement to the pipe boys, as well as comforted their people who came into the office to say hello but were really miss-ing their loved ones out on the pipe who were gone for months at a time. This job was tough on the pipe boys, but also for their families, and Millie understood. Will was right: Millie was the heart of the office. Her love for her boys was genuine, and Zander was becoming one in her fold.

"Ahh, here we are. The last of these sizes. I'll put in an order today for more." A pile of fall and winter clothing and boots had been put together for Zander. All had that logo embroidered on them, a logo he thought he had gotten away from.

"You boys always get tears, snags, lose your clothing somewhere out there. A shirt becomes a makeshift rag in a pinch when one of those machines you bounce around on," meaning the four-wheelers and snow machines, "needs some oil. Just remember," she said, turning to Zander holding out a jacket to him, "Baking soda and whiskey gets almost everything out."

Zander nodded as he took the jacket and slipped it on.

"Fits you like a glove, love!" Millie exclaimed as she ran her hands along Zander's arms, raising them and making sure he had enough room to move.

"And there's a bit of extra room if you need to put on another layer underneath."

Zander was not used to all the fuss Millie was making or used to another person being so close to him, let alone touching him. He took some deep breaths. Millie noticed this and stopped her fussing. She looked up at him; the top of her head barely reached his shoulders. She put out her hands. which were small and warm, and placed them on his cheeks, cradling his head in her hands. Her eyes looked up into his. "Hon, I can outfit you and make sure you have what you need to weather the storms out there. Even though you don't say much, your eyes reflect the gales you are dealing with. I can't prepare you for those."

She let go of Zander's face and he hung his head.

Zander followed the pipe road. He had loaded up his gear on the back of the four-wheeler and slid his rifle into the side-mounted gun rack. He stopped for a moment on a crest to look down to the town below and then up at the mountain beyond. The easy glide of a raptor caught his eye, a Gyrfalcon. He had miles to travel on his own. Zander radioed in his starting mile and Will's voice came back. "Copy."

Then he heard the clicks of the other pipe boys saying, "Copy." this was their way of welcoming him to the team.

The final click was from Chip. "Copy that. You have a good ride out there."

And then all was silent. Zander breathed in, then started up the four-wheeler and took off over the trail alongside the pipe.

The pipe boys rode up one side of the pipe along their designated mile markers. The policy was that every fifteen miles they were expected to radio in, so that if something happened to them, it narrowed down the search field. Once the pipe boys reached their final markers, they'd loop under the pipe and travel along the opposite side of the trail head back down the mile markers. Along their rides, as Will showed Zander, they were expected to log any discrepancies or disturbances. The travel along the pipe wasn't a race. No matter how quickly the pipe boys far north of the borough made it up and back along their mile markers, they were expected to loop again and again until their eight months or four months on the pipe were finished. Zander and Will's loop was the closest to town, and therefore Zander would be able to go into town after he made his first loop.

So far, the fall had been mild, but the weather in this land shifted at a moment's notice. Zander was prepared. The uniforms were warm and comfortable and did a great job of shielding him from the elements. The mild days at the beginning of his eight-four turned swiftly. Zander, who had looked forward to sleeping out at night with a blazing fire, had to switch his plans a few nights and stay in one of the guard shacks along the way. Standing in the one-room shanty heating up soup, looking out the window and listening to the wind, his mind drifted to her, and he'd catch himself. He'd shake his head, as if that would throw the thought permanently out of his mind. He set up a little workstation on the table with his bowl of soup. He wrote in his logged miles; he reviewed the notes of disturbances he saw. There were a few trees down in one area, which seemed odd to him, so he indicated that on his map to circle back to when coming back down the pipe. He looked out the window, as the wind rattled the thin boards of the shack. In the distance he heard wolves howl, and he knew that somewhere there was something or someone who would not see the morning.

Zander had already made one full loop of his leg of the pipe. He slid into the hanger on his four-wheeler as the snow and ice arrived. The other pipe boys farther north would load up a truck and trailer with both a four-wheeler and snow machine and secure them along the pipe to switch for the seasons. But Zander knew he would make good time on the pipe and would be able to arrive at the office to switch machines. He flashed his badge at the side door and went into the office, carrying his laundry bag. The building was dark except for a light in the office where Millie was finishing up some filing. Zander gave her a nod as he headed for the supply room. As he pulled some blank log sheets and pens from their places on the shelves, Millie spoke. "All set up there?" she asked.

"Hmmm," Zander replied.

Millie shook her head with a slight smile on her face. She continued, "You working things out?"

Zander paused, then walked to the doorway. Millie stopped her filing and turned to him. "Snow came fast this time. Mountains seems to be bothered by something." She looked at Zander over the rim of her glasses, "or someone."

Zander leaned on the doorframe, looking down and to the side. He hadn't heard anyone speak that much in two months, and he wasn't sure of his words.

Millie eyed the laundry bag. "I bet those smell ripe," she teased. "Just put them in the cart. The laundry service will pick them up tomorrow."

He turned and picked up the bag that held his dirty clothes and placed it in the cart just inside the room where the clothing locker was.

"I ordered more clothing in your size. Thought you might be in sometime this week. I put what I think you might need on the bench in there." Millie turned back to the filing cabinet and pushed it closed.

Zander picked up the clothing; there was enough to last him a few months. He could hear Millie walking across the office. He called from where he stood, "Thank you, Millie."

Millie poked her head in the doorway, looking at Zander. "You're welcome, my boy. Now, go see if you can calm the mountains." Millie pushed off the doorframe and headed out to her desk. Grabbing her purse, she shut off her desk light, flashed her badge, and pushed through the door to the parking lot.

As Zander rode past Emil's house, he saw the lights on in the kitchen. He could stay the night, as Will had said was an option for their leg on the pipe, but Zander kept riding.

The days along the pipe blended into one another. Zander had no use for remembering days of the week. In this world, where he was the only person around, he needed to remember to be vigilant, to log in the miles, and radio in his position on the pipe. He took note of the conditions of the shacks along his route. He inventoried their supplies, observing the expiration dates on the food. He stopped and ran his hands along the metal pipe with its vast circumference. He remembered certain places; knew he had been there before. He remembered his family being here, on this land.

During the day, he took note of the tracks left behind by wolves, moose, caribou, and rabbits. He was observant of any tracks from vehicles or persons that were not from the pipe boys. Above him, he saw hawks and eagles in flight. He looked to the tree lines for anything out of the ordinary. At night, he listened to the mountains, to the land, to the howls of the wolves, and the hoot of owls, and held her sweater in his hands.

Other than the clicks and check-ins from the other pipe boys rolling over the walkies and the familiar voice of Will confirming their words, Zander heard no other voices and didn't see another person for months.

One day, the weather turned rapidly, the wind and snow battered Zander and made it difficult to see. He had planned to put more miles under him, but instead he took refuge in the closest shack. The night was a restless one, the wind sounding as if it were ripping the roof right off the shack, and Zander couldn't get his mind to quiet. The next morning, outside the door and around the perimeter of the shack, Zander observed a lone wolf's tracks.

When he reached his end marker, Zander stood off
of the snow machine and looked up the pipe. Milo was
somewhere off in the distance and should be radioing
in soon. Zander took his walkie in his hand and called
in his last mile marker.

"Heading back."

"Copy," Will said.

Zander went back to the snow machine, started it
up, and ducked under the raised platform that lifted the
pipe up over the hill and began to travel down the other
side of the pipe, observing and looking for anything that
needed to be logged and addressed.

It was the end of March. Zander stood in the lobby looking out the floor-to-ceiling glass windows. This was his second check-in at the office in the five months he'd been out on the pipe. The glass front of the building gave great views of the town's straight and wide and all the towns' happenings. Zander watched as the snow fell, and trucks and cars rolled up and down the straight and wide. He looked to the General Store to see if Emil's truck was parked out front. It wasn't. He would stay at Emil's for the night, sleeping in his old bed, before leaving again for his last three months on the pipe. He caught sight of Will leaving the General Store, carrying some bags and a box. Through the snow, Zander thought he caught a glimpse of a familiar logo on the side of the white box before it was placed in the bed of a pickup truck. Zander went to shift his gaze, thinking nothing of it, when he saw another figure put a bag in the bed of the same truck. Zander had been running the blade of his knife over the top of his thumb. He had sharpened it the evening before after deciding it was too dull. He watched the two figures talk for a while and then he saw it. A movement he couldn't forget—the woman raised her arm and, with her hand, brushed a long strand of hair out of her face. At this movement, the blade of his knife sliced his thumb. He winced. *No, it couldn't be,* he thought. He looked down for a second and saw a bead of red blood form. He looked up again. Will was riding his snow machine toward the office. The other figure watched for a moment, and then went back into the General Store. After parking his machine next to Zander's, Will walked through the door, brushing the snow from his uniform. Eyeing Zander, a smile came to his face.

"You're making good time. How's it going?"

"Hmmm," Zander mumbled.

Will knew to interpret that as fine. He turned to Millie, "Any messages?"

"Nope. I'm just finishing up this week's paperwork for you and then I'll be leaving."

Zander followed Will down the hall to their office. Will took off his jacket and hung it on the coat rack. Will knew how the conversation was going to play out, but he had promised Christine. "Hey, Christine's putting together a dinner for some of the pipe boys who are in town. We'd like it if you could make it," Will offered.

Zander stood there forming the words in his mind. Finally, he said, "I appreciate it, maybe next time."

"Okay then," Will replied and turned his attention to the whiteboard. Zander leaned against the front of his desk looking down at his bleeding thumb. "Who was that you were just talking to?"

"Millie?" Will asked quizzically.

Zander tilted his head to the side.

"Oh, you mean at the store," Will said.

Zander nodded.

"She's the new veterinarian. She seems nice enough," Will answered. Chip came out of the copier room carrying a stack of blank log sheets for his binder. "She's pretty cute too," he chimed in. Will, who had his back to the room, turned and took notice of Chip putting the blank pages into the binder. Will turned back to the whiteboard and wrote in the last logged markers for the pipe boys still out on their legs.

"I thought you were dating Amber. What's up with you checking out other women?" Will asked, then turned back to the room to find only Zander in it. Zander motioned with his head to the break room where Chip had gone. Will looked toward the door, but there was no answer. Will continued, "I found out she's not seasonal. She's moved up here permanently." Chip came out of the break room carrying an apple and handed a bandage to Zander, who gave an upturned nod as a thanks to Chip.

"Yeah, I may be with Amber, but that doesn't stop me from being observant. That is a major part of our jobs, observing," Chip emphasized.

Zander looked at Will, who had now turned around again. "He's got you there."

"Anyway," Will said, annoyed, putting the cap on the marker, "she's moved up in the mountains. Into one of those vacation homes that was for sale."

"When I was out doing rounds a couple of weeks ago, I radioed the folks, and they asked me to check in on her. She seemed a bit snow shocked with all that the storms brought; not sure she was ready for that," Chip said.

"Well, she's ready now," Will said, sitting down in his chair. "She's got enough food for weeks; she bought a CB radio—"

"That was my idea, I told her to get that," Chip cut in with the look of a proud five-year-old who just got a gold star on a drawing.

Will continued, "and she bought breakup gear, so I don't think she was scared off."

Millie came into the room and put a stack of paperwork on Will's desk. "I'm leaving for the night."

In unison the three said, "Bye, Millie."

As she hit the doorway, she turned and looked over her glasses that rested on the bridge of her nose. "Oh, and you boys might want to take this conversation to the corner. Nighty-night."

Will chuckled, Zander felt the warmth in his face and focused on his bandage, and Chip rolled his eyes. They all knew the corner was the nickname for the gossip hangout in town at the General Store, where the locals and known travelers to the area went to catch up on anything or anyone worthy of discussing.

"How come she can hear all that, but when she's ordering lunch, she never hears me say I want lunch?" Chip asked.

"Chip, watch it or I'll tell your mother," Millie yelled from the lobby.

"See," Chip said as he pointed a finger at the door with a wide-eyed look. Zander shook his head while Will smirked. "Well, I'm going to head out and do some work." Chip tucked the binder under his arm after he pushed off the desk.

"I'm going to stay the night, then I'm off," Zander said. "I'll radio when I hit the marker."

"Be safe," Will called after Zander and turned his attention to the paperwork before him. Zander and Chip walked out to the lobby and saw Millie drive out of the parking lot heading for her home.

"See you, Zander," Chip said as he climbed on his snow machine and tore off down the straight and wide.

Zander started up his own machine. He pulled on his goggles and headed toward Emil's house.

Emil noticed a break in the falling snow and took the opportunity to go out to the woodpile and bring in some more wood for the fire. Outside, he heard the engine of a snow machine and looked to the end of his driveway. There he made out a black snow machine with a rider. He continued to put logs in the crook of his elbow. Zander shut off the sled, then joined Emil at the woodpile and began piling wood in his arms. They walked back inside, kicking and stomping the snow off their boots. Zander followed Emil to the living room, where a warm fire blazed. Emil knelt in front of the fire while Zander piled his logs onto the others, then he went to Mishka who waited patiently for attention. Zander scratched behind the dog's ears and under her chin as Emil stroked the fire. The silence finally getting to him he asked, "Everything good up on the pipe?"

"Hmmm," Zander said, straightening up. "Anything I should know?" he asked, still waiting for his past to catch up to him.

"No," Emil said, slowly shaking his head. Outside the snow was picking up again. Once Zander made it to the doorway, Emil turned his head sideways. While holding a log and shaking it up and down, he said, "Oh wait." Zander stopped, his back to Emil. "I went to visit Gus the other day. He had a steer that needed stitches because another steer gored him. Apparently, we have a new veterinarian in town, a female. She bought the property that runs along the 456. She had just left Gus's when I got there." He paused, and Zander held his breath. "She makes a tight stitch."

Zander's eyes pressed closed, his jaw clenched. His hand went to his side, the side where he remembered her hand touching him. He remembered her face, her concentration as she studied his wound, and as she sewed one stitch after the other. Emil threw the log on the fire as Zander disappeared out into the snow.

Standing in the entryway to his house, Will heard the lovely hum of his wife Christine coming from the kitchen. He shut the front door, calling out a hello to her as he took off his coat. He went down the hall to join her in the kitchen. Will didn't take Zander's rejection for dinner as badly as Christine.

"He's a loner, love, and I think he wants to stay that way," Will said, trying to ease his wife's disappointment.

"It's only dinner. We're not asking him to move in," Christine said with a pout.

Will put his arm around Christine's waist. "You're a kind person, one of the reasons I love you, but some people aren't meant to be around others and that's okay."

"Do you think that's why he said no because there will be other pipe boys? Should we maybe just ask him over? We could do that!" She perked up with excitement at the prospect.

Will sighed. She was also persistent, another thing he loved about her, but Will knew the size of the guest list wouldn't make a difference with Zander. He kissed her head as she stirred what was in the saucepan. "Sure, love, I'll ask him again when he's down from the pipe if he'd like to come over with just us." Christine turned her head and kissed Will; she was smiling and went back to humming.

Chip had done the rounds in town and would soon head to the outlying houses for some check-ins. Everything had been pretty quiet in the town. He headed over to the General Store to say hi to his parents and let them know he'd be around for dinner. He went through the door, the sleigh bells clanged, and he brushed the snow off of his shoulders and turned to the corner. There were few people there, as it was close to closing time. Chip waved and said, "Hello." He turned to the counter where he saw his parents doing the receipts and counting the register drawer. Chip went over to them.

"Hey, Mom and Pop. So, after I head up and check in on some of the outliers, I can swing back around and be home for dinner."

Chip's mother Dika smiled. "That sounds good, Chip, It'll be nice to have you home for dinner."

Patuk asked, "How are things going?"

"Good, you know, busy. We're still removing snow from the pipe in places, but it's been quiet," Chip replied.

Dika looked up from the piles of receipts. "You missed Waverly, she was just in here a little while ago. You know she's a nice woman. Single." Dika didn't approve of the girls Chip had been involved with and let him know it.

"Ma, she's like older."

"Sometimes older can be advantageous. More stable, more confident, wiser," chimed in Patuk.

"Sure," Chip said, "but I'm pretty sure she's spoken for."

"She moved up here alone. I haven't heard of her being seen with anyone." Patuk said. "Who?" Looking at his son, he recognized all too well that *I know something you don't know* look on his face.

"Zander. I think he's interested in her," Chip said in a hushed voice.

Dika raised her head again. "Who's this now?"

Chip rolled his eyes. "How is it that you two are here every day, with the corner less than fifty feet away, and you don't know the town gossip?"

"Well, we are working, Chip. It's not like we sit back there," Patuk responded.

Dika broke in. "So, who is this Zander?"

"You know him, Zander, the kid Emil took in. He's the guy who took Craig's position on the pipe."

Patuk and Dika looked at each other.

"What?" Chip asked.

"We were just talking about him," Patuk said. "We were just talking about him after years of forgetting about him."

"Who were you talking about him to? Someone came in asking about him?" asked Chip.

"Oh no, not a stranger. We wouldn't discuss history with a stranger. No, it was Waverly," replied Dika.

"See, told you she's spoken for," Chip said.

"Well, she wasn't exactly asking about him. She asked about Will and who and what he does. He helped her carry her purchases out to her truck. She's a bit wary of strangers. We told her about you pipe boys and a little bit about what you do on the pipe and here in town. Then she asked about the logo, and we told her how Zander designed that," Dika explained.

"Did you mention his name?" asked Chip.

"I don't remember," Patuk said.

Dika and Chip looked at him with a mockingly shocked look. Dika responded, "We said Emil took him in as a boy and gave him an Athabaskan name, Reins. I can't believe he's come back."

"He's been back. He's been up at the lodge for a meet, he's working the eight-four, and he just stopped in the office," Chip said. "Making his second full loop."

"Does Emil know?" asked Dika.

"Of course, he knows. Zander's been staying with him," replied Chip.

Dika wanted to ask more questions, but Patuk was more interested in his son. "Are you going to be bringing Veronica with you to dinner?" asked Patuk.

Chip was pulling on his gloves and heading to the door. He turned, shaking his head at his father and mother. "Really?" he asked sarcastically. "That's old news. I'm now with Amber. And no, it'll just be me, your amazing son, coming to dinner tonight."

He went through the door and got on his sled, heading out of town to the outliers to do his check-ins. He was shaking his head, wondering how his parents were so oblivious to the local changes and the changes within their own son's life, but then again, he could barely keep track of his girlfriends. He traveled the straight and wide heading out of town.

The last of the customers left the General Store. Patuk and Dika closed up for the night. Dika said to Patuk as they walked to their truck, "I can't believe he's come back."

Patuk thought she was talking about their son coming for dinner. "He'd never miss a meal, you know that. I'm just glad he's not with what's her name anymore. She's nothing but trouble."

"I was talking about that boy, Zander being back, and her name is Veronica."

"Oh," Patuk said.

"When the Blakes moved up here, they were all close, them, Emil, and Charlie Jewett. Remember him, he was working his way up the pipe's company ladder?" Dika remembered.

"I remember they were all good friends, enough to get those perpetual terms from Charlie, but I guess I never put much thought into the boy after he was sent away," Patuk said.

"What do you think it means, him coming back?" asked Dika.

"I think it means more that Emil didn't share it with all of us," Patuk responded.

Dika nodded in agreement while Patuk looked out the window at the night sky. The moon had a distinct ring around it.

"Oh, hey Zander. You're just in time to help me with this delivery," Will said. Zander had finished backing up a truck and trailer and had put fuel in his quad. He had stayed a bit longer in town this trip. The spring breakup had turned to flooding in some areas, and the pipe boys were needed to help with sandbagging, rerouting the runoff from the rivers that headed for homes, and putting up detours for the traffic going in and out of town. He would be leaving soon to complete his last few months on the pipe. They headed out and around the corner of the building and met up with a truck and horse trailer by the stables.

"We getting a new mount?" Zander asked.

"No, this one belongs to the vet," Will replied.

In the waning light, Zander saw the white speckles on a grey rump of a horse. Will swung open the back of the trailer. The horse snorted anxiously. Will went to take a step in, and Zander could tell he was hesitant.

"You go deal with the driver," Zander said as he pulled himself up into the trailer by a metal bar on the side.

Will headed to the driver of the rig, who had a clipboard with a stack of paperwork on it. The horse pranced in place as Zander whispered to it. The horse's bridle was just loose enough to allow her to turn her head and eye this person coming at her. Once she saw Zander, she stopped prancing and bowed her head in recognition.

"Hey there, Thistle. You've come a long way."

Zander unhooked the bridle and backed Thistle up. She hesitated at the drop of the step, but Zander rubbed her nose. "Slow," he whispered, and she put one foot out of the trailer. Once clear of the door he turned her and brought her into the warm stable where the boys' mounts were busy eating hay. Will closed the trailer's door. He was holding a stack of paperwork and left it on the bales of hay by the stable's doorway.

"Nice looking horse," Will commented.

"She's an Appaloosa," Zander replied.

"Well, she must mean something to the vet. She shipped her here."

Zander was opening a bale of hay and spreading it loose for Thistle.

"Care to make a wager?" Will asked.

"Is there anything you won't bet on?" Zander replied.

Will looked for a moment at the wall, "I don't think so," he said laughing.

"Let's hear it."

"I bet you a hundred bucks that Waverly named this horse something like Sprinkles."

Zander laughed, "Alright, I'll take that bet. I'll go with Thistle."

"Thistle! That's a plant, not a name," Will laughed. "Well, tomorrow I'll find out when I deliver her. I'm gonna head home. Have a good night."

"Night," Zander said as he patted Thistle, laughing to himself. He picked up the stack of paperwork, brought it into the main building, and placed it on Will's desk before leaving again for the pipe.

Either due to weather or someone removing them, a few no-trespassing signs needed to be reposted. Zander made note and looked for any tracks nearby. From his pack, he pulled a few no-trespassing signs that had the company's name and logo on them and posted them in place. He continued on his way.

Zander would look for anything alongside the pipe that shouldn't be there—dents, graffiti, damage—and he would continue to observe the tracks of animals. On this leg, when Zander hit the 456 marker, he found himself noticing the no-trespassing signs were either missing or faded and thought that he would need to get those replaced. Then it hit him: he had found himself caring about the land and wanting to protect it. It was the first time he had thought about the land as his.

"Zander at the 456," he said over the walkie.

"Copy," Will responded. "Hey Zander, can you make a quick stop and check in on the veterinarian up there right along that marker? The ramblers have been coming through, and with all the Midnight Sun Celebration commotion here in town, I haven't been able to check on her."

The words Will was saying came through the walkie in his hand, and Zander looked to the tree line. Just a little way off was the distinct possibility that she was there. He had been struggling with this possibility, and not just the possibility of it being her and wanting it to be her, but how could it be her? He had put thousands of miles between them. How could she be here? And then that tugging question, Why was she here? That was his mind, but his heart . . . in his heart, he wanted to be with her.

"Zander? You copy?" Will asked over the walkie.

Zander nodded, still looking at the pines, then pressed the button with his thumb. "Copy."

"Great, thanks man."

Up on a ridge, Chip sat on jutting rocks looking out, a pair of binoculars focused on the plain below and watching a caribou prance across a stream. He was listening to the radio chatter and holding his breath, waiting for Zander to respond. Chip considered himself a bit of a Don Juan or Casanova with the ladies, but deep down he was a romantic. When he heard the request from Will, Chip couldn't contain himself. He turned up the volume on his walkie and waited silently. This could be Zander's chance to speak with Waverly. Chip found it so odd that a man of Zander's confidence was so unsure of himself when it came to Waverly. When, finally, Zander's single spoken word "Copy" came through, Chip raised an arm in the air and called out, "Yes!" His word echoed down to the caribou who stopped, hoof in mid-air. The animal turned its head in Chip's direction. Chip, in his enthusiasm, teetered off the rocky post and fell to the ground, laughing and smiling as he looked up at the sky. The caribou, taking Chip as no threat, continued prancing across the stream and into the brush beyond.

Zander sat on his quad for a bit, looking down at his hands. The evening was still light, as the summer hours and the Alaskan sun intertwined. Zander took off through the pines, weaving in and out of the trees. When he saw the trees get thinner and the aspens begin to crop up, he killed the quad's engine. He sat for a moment, listening. The night was still. Miles up the pipe he had seen the tracks of the horses used by the ramblers and the tracks of their cattle. Some of the ramblers, who were rougher than the others, the ones who didn't abide by the private property or no-trespassing signs, would sometimes go through others' land and were not always the most respectful of other people's property or the people who owned the property. He got off of his quad and made his way to the clearing. He saw the barn, where he knew Thistle slept. He went down along the back of the barn and listened again. He heard the rustle of Thistle, but nothing else. He went around the front and checked the door to the barn; it was snugly shut and locked. He looked to the house. She had chosen a beautiful home and location. He stood still, looking for any sign of movement. He heard a twig break somewhere in the woods and he focused his eyes. He saw a flash of brown. *Just a chipmunk.* He walked over to the drive and stole a glance at her truck and, inside, he saw her medical bag. It was remarkably similar to the one she had with her that night in the kitchen. He looked to the front door of her home; it was only a few easy strides for him. How easy it would be to walk up to that porch and knock on her door, but not easy for him. He moved away, back toward the woods and his quad. He stood there, leaning up against a pine mixed in with the aspens.

Then he saw her. She came out of the house slowly, holding the screen door with one hand and looking out onto the porch. He felt himself straighten. She let the door go and walked out onto the porch. She looked to the barn, then out at the end of the drive, then to the woods. She was looking in his direction but made no gesture of seeing him. He held still, watching her. Her bare feet moved across the boards of the porch and her arms hung at her sides until the breeze blew errant strands of hair across her face and she reached up to move them out of her eyes, still looking in his direction. The breeze fluttered her nightgown around her knees. She turned and went back inside. The still night had changed, now a constant breeze was blowing. Zander stood there listening to the aspens. He turned and went back to his quad, started up the engine, and headed back to the pipe. When he reached the trail, he radioed in. "Zander, marker 456," and added, "all clear."

Chip, who was now walking down the rocky trail, stopped and said, rather loudly, "What?" with a look of disbelief on his face, staring at the walkie talkie in his hand. Chip knew there was no way that Zander has spoken to her in that small amount of time.

Will copied, then added, "Hey, Zander, I'm going to need all hands for the Midnight Sun Celebration. You gonna make it back to town tonight?"

"Affirmative," Zander said.

Will went back to reviewing the several permits on his desk for the Midnight Sun Celebration.

Zander moved down the rest of the pipe, checking in at the mile markers. Darkness settled in, and Zander turned on the quad's headlights as he approached the 442. His eyes caught something dangling in the breeze. The wind began to blow whatever it was frantically, as if to say, "Here, look at me." Zander let the quad idle as he pulled up to the marker. He reached out, caught the object in his hand, and looked at it. There, woven into leather string, were three buttons. He clenched them in his hand, looking back up the pipe to where she was. The wind died down, and he turned to look toward the town. The lone wolf he suspected of following him about sat there in front of him in the headlights. It raised itself and began walking toward Zander. It leaped up the little cliff where Zander sat on his quad. Zander watched the wolf get nearer to him, moving gingerly by him. It turned its head to look at Zander and their eyes met. A lone howl was heard in the distance up the pipe, and the wolf trotted in that direction, away from Zander. He wrapped the leather string around his wrist and maneuvered the quad down the slope to town.

After filling the quad up with fuel, he drove it into the hanger. As he was taking off his packs and grabbing his gear from the vehicle, Chip rode in. As they headed into the main building together, Will was on his way out. "I'm heading home. Chip, you got the radio tonight?"

"I sure do," Chip replied.

Will said his good nights. He knew that with the Midnight Sun Celebration events he'd be pretty busy, and he wanted to enjoy some time at home with Christine.

Zander was busy logging in miles next to his name on the whiteboard while Chip leaned against his desk, watching. Zander felt eyes burning into the back of his head, so he turned and looked at Chip. He raised his eyebrows with a questioning look.

"Did you speak with her?" Chip questioned.

Zander turned back to the board, "Who?" he mumbled.

"Waverly," Chip said importantly.

"No," Zander replied bluntly.

"Why not?" Chip asked, flailing his hands in the air.

Zander, putting the last few notes on the whiteboard, shrugged his shoulders. He put the cap on the dry-erase marker and turned around, the room was empty. He put the keys to his quad on the hook on the side of his desk and removed his truck keys, then headed out the door. Sitting behind the wheel, he put the key in the ignition and looked at the leather string around his wrist. He started the truck, pulled out of the parking lot, and headed up the mountain to Emil's house.

He half expected Emil to be sitting at the table awake and waiting for him, but the house was dark. Mishka came over to him from her mat in the kitchen. Zander pet and scratched her, got a glass of water, and headed up the stairs to his room. Once inside, he got undressed and headed for the shower. He unwound the leather string from his wrist and laid it on the edge of the sink. His mind went back to seeing her on the porch. She had deliberately put the buttons on that marker. She had kept them. Once out of the shower, he dried off and slipped on some boxers and, taking the leather string and buttons with him, he crawled into bed. He wrapped them around his wrist once again, and, feeling the buttons with his fingers, he looked out into the summer night sky. Slowly his eyes began to close, and sleep came to him.

He awoke the next day in the late morning. He pulled
on a pair of pants and a shirt and went downstairs. He
could hear Emil in the kitchen moving things around.
Zander came into the kitchen, rubbing an eye with the
palm of one hand.

"You're up," Emil said.

Zander took notice of what Emil was doing, but it
didn't make sense to him. Bags of feathers, glue sticks,
pipe cleaners, and small scissors with brightly colored
handles along with dry pasta in bags were strewn on
the table. Emil followed Zander's gaze.

"I'm in charge of one of the craft tables for the kid-
dies at the Agri-Center this year for the Midnight Sun
Celebration," Emil explained.

Zander stood in front of the table, nodding as now the random items made sense.

"So, you got called in? You made good time on the pipe then. Anything on the pipe to report?" asked Emil.

"Hmmm," Zander said, shaking his head. He was filling up a coffee cup from the pot. Replacing it on the burner, he turned and faced the kitchen and Emil who was packing up more items for the crafting. "Can you get me some of those no-trespassing signs?"

"Don't you boys have your own for the pipe?"

"It's not for the pipe land," Zander responded.

Emil stopped what he was doing and turned slightly to Zander, realizing he was talking about the Blake property. "I'll do it this afternoon when I head into town. I'll stop at Town Hall and get them."

"Thanks." Zander pushed off the counter and headed back up the stairs to his room.

He dressed and readied for work. Back in the kitchen, Emil felt happy. Zander had at least acknowledged his family's property. Zander came back down the stairs and patted Mishka.

"I made you a sandwich." Emil handed him the brown paper bag with his lunch in it. Zander took the bag and headed outside to his truck.

Millie said good morning as Zander came through the main office door. "Morning," he replied and walked through to their desks. Will was there with both Chip and Welch.

"This year's Midnight Sun Celebration will be larger than previous years, at least according to the permits I've had to approve," said Will. "Welch, you good with the southern part of the straight and wide?"

"Yes, sir. I double checked the posted signs for truck and traffic detours," Welch reported. "The regular truckers are used to this time of year, but the rookies I think will fall in line. Westie was here shortly after the pass was cleared, doing a short stint. On his way back down, he said he'd radio the others and let them know to take the western route," Welch stated.

"Great. Chip, parking detail," Will said.

"All set with posted signs for no street parking starting tomorrow at 4 a.m. The back parking lots have been cleared and are ready for overflow from the regular public parking areas," replied Chip.

"Alright. We will be doing crowd control as well. Watch for the brawlers and the bruisers, we all know who the locals are, but this event always draws others," cautioned Will. "Lastly, Zander, I figured you might want to stay here and man the radio, keep track of the logs?"

Zander breathed a sigh of relief. "Got it," he confirmed.

"Everybody stay safe. Remember, we're here as seconds to law enforcement, but if you see anything you radio and get on it. Alright, let's head out."

Welch, Chip, and Will headed out into town. Millie was packing up. Zander settled in and waited for the check-ins from the boys on the pipe to come over the walkies.

"Well, you missed an excellent Midnight Sun Celebration, man. The vendors couldn't get enough of us and our help, so appreciative. I'm stuffed. How's it been?" Welch asked Zander.

Zander stood up and stretched. "Quiet. Marty's bunkered down at the 1040 and Milo is in the guard shack off the eights because his back hurts and he doesn't want to sleep on the ground."

Welch shook his head. "He needs to toughen up. Will sent me back here to take over. The vendors are all packed up and I got all the barricades and detour signs taken down. You gonna head into town for a few on-the-house rounds? Those bars are crankin'."

Zander shook his head. "I'll see you in a few hours."

Zander scanned his ID at the screen and pushed his way through the main door. In the parking lot, the light from the sun's solstice gave a warm glow around the land. Zander closed his eyes as a breeze shifted his gaze up the mountains. He reached in his pocket, took out the keys to the quad, and headed to the hanger. He got on the machine and headed up the pipe, passing marker after marker. In the nightless night sky, a Gyrfalcon trailed along after Zander.

When he came to the 456, he turned right and went into the pines. He saw the clearing ahead with the aspens and he pulled up to the back of the house. He didn't see her truck in the drive. He went up on to the porch and walked around to the part facing town. He looked out at the view and the town below, the lights twinkling. He saw a pair of headlights making their way up the road and then pull into her drive. He spun around to be on the back wall of the porch, facing the tree line. He listened to her truck come to a stop, the engine shut off, the door opening and then closing. He closed his eyes and remembered her mouth. He heard her footsteps on the porch. When he opened his eyes, her footsteps had stopped. Then he heard her move toward the door and he rolled his shoulder around the corner. She was almost to the door. His heart was in his throat, and he cleared it. She dropped her keys and turned to him. He could make out her face, her eyes looking right at him. He couldn't believe that she was right there. He heard her words, and for a moment he didn't want to move, afraid that he wasn't the reason she was on this porch.

She asked him a question. . . . Yes, he had found the buttons. He loosened the leather from his wrist and let them dangle for her to see. He pushed off the side of the house and walked closer to her. He felt his knees weaken and he went to the porch railing closest to her. He watched her watch him. He breathed in once his hands made it to the railing. He let his head fall a bit, and he heard her say something else about the eight-four. He mumbled a response. He didn't understand why she had such an effect on him. Chance encounters, a tragic night, and now she was right there within arm's reach. He lifted his head; he heard her speak again and then stop. He looked out to the mountain; in the distance he heard two wolves howling. He hung his head again. He saw her move out of the corner of his eye.

"I wanted you to come. I wanted you here with me," he said as he pushed off the rail and turned to her. She was still. He walked over to her, and his left hand holding the leather string with the buttons went to her waist. He moved his hand over her curves and to the small of her back. His right hand went up to her neck and moved along her jawline.

"I wanted you to come. I wanted you here, with me."

His left hand gripped some of the material from the back of her dress and he pulled her against his body. He looked into her eyes and then felt her lips on his.